PLAYING THE ODDS

MILTON J. DAVIS

MVmedia, LLC
Fayetteville, GA

MVmedia, LLC
PO Box 1465
Fayetteville, GA 30214
www.mvmediaatl.com

Publisher's Note: This is a work of fiction. Names, characters, places, and incidents are a product of the author's imagination. Locales and public names are sometimes used for atmospheric purposes. Any resemblance to actual people, living or dead, or to businesses, companies, events, institutions, or locales is completely coincidental.

Book Layout ©2017 BookDesignTemplates.com
Cover Art by Sean Hill

Ordering Information:
Quantity sales. Special discounts are available on quantity purchases by corporations, associations, and others. For details, contact the "Special Sales Department" at the address above.

Playing the Odds/Milton J. Davis. -- 1st ed.
ISBN no. 978-1-7372277-9-3

CONTENTS

Dedication to the Cyberfunkateers. The future is ours.

EPISODE ONE:
REPOSSESSION BLUES

I should have known better. After twenty years on the grind there's little I haven't seen, done, or run away from. But old habits are hard to break, and there's always the possibility that things might actually turn out right. So, when the lights came on and illuminated the room full of killers, I was disappointed but not surprised. Some skinny guy dressed in a tailor-made suit that was more expensive than he deserved sat behind the desk. Celia, the woman who led me into this trap, stood behind him, flashing that alluring smile and perfect body that convinced me to take a chance.

Unfortunately for them my guns were fully charged, and my battle tech had already calculated the optimum fire pattern. I would sustain 20% maximum damage and I could handle that. I felt bad about Celia though; she was kind of cute. But business is business. I cut down the slick suit first, a bolt in the forehand. The meat bag beside me got a round off that grazed my shoulder before I put him down with a bolt between the eyes. The others went down with various lethal punc-tures wounds while I took another round to the thigh and one to the ribs. The nanos were healing me before I low-ered my bolters and my hand sleeves slid back into place. Celia was in shock, Suit Boy's blood splattered on her nice blouse and tight skirt. I altered the battle tech

kill zone to drop her from the sweep, because I'm a
softy. I gave her my best smile.

"That offer to your place still on?" I asked.

My voice snapped her out of her daze. She
looked around the room then let out a scream that almost
shattered my eardrums. Celia shoved me out of the way
and into the wall as she sprinted like a track droid out the
room.

"I guess that's a no," I said.

I limped out of the basement back into the rave.
The music pounded my head as I made my way to the
exit, the ravers blissfully unaware of what went down
beneath their dancing feet. I didn't waste any thought
about who my ambushers were or why they were after
me; the list of meat bags that wanted my ass dead was
too long, and I didn't care. Comes with the business.
That's why I stay sharp and upgraded. The best tech will
keep you above ground. The first thing I learned. My
contact with Cytech kept me pumped with the latest, and
even a few experimental additions.

My EV was waiting when I stepped out on the
curb. I hopped in and it merged into the level 7 traffic.
Aytee-El was beautiful at night, the lights of synchro-
nized EV and scooters flowing between the illuminated
scrapers like blood through an organic. Man, I loved that
city.

I was settling into the ride when my cell blinked.
Dedren Carmichael's profile filled my screen and I
frowned. I'm signed up with three corporations; Cytech,
the cybernetic tech powerhouse; Robins, Tyler and Tate,
Interplanetary Law Firm; and Triad Enterprises, a little
firm that did a bit of everything but nothing very well.
Triad was Dedren's company. I don't know how the man
stayed in business, but he did. He was also the most an-
noying of my clients. I let him hang as I checked my vitals. The nannies were doing their job; I should be fully

repaired by the time I reached my flat. I picked up the comm and put on a fake smile.

"What's up, Dedren?"

Dedren brushed back the hair on his forehead and flashed his big-toothed grin. The man was a cryptonaire and wouldn't spend a chit for hair stim.

"Just checking in on my investment," he said. "You seem a bit flushed."

"Nah, I'm good. Just a little extra-curricular activity," I said with a grin. That was Dedren's gift. The man was beyond perceptive. Maybe that was what he spent his crypts on. It was illegal, but rich bags don't care. That's why they're rich.

"Look, I was thinking you could stop by for a visit," he said. "I have some things I'd like to . . ."

The comm went black. I cursed; I was being hacked. I was trying to recall if I left anyone alive from the shootout when the universal emblem of Milky Way Savings and Trust filled my screen.

"Please stand by for a Priority Five Message," the syrupy southern voice said. "And thank you for choosing Milky Way Savings and Trust for your worldwide financial needs."

The pleasant brown face of a stately looking woman appeared.

"Hello, I'm Diane Freeman. Is this Carlos Mejia?"

"That's me," I said.

"Carlos Mejia, this call is to inform you that your employer, Cytech, Inc., has filed for Chapter 7 bankruptcy under the laws of the United Cities Federation. As a result of this action, all properties of the company are to be gathered and liquidated at three crypts on the c-dollar. Please remain where you are for imminent collection."

I was terrified.

"Wait . . . what?" Collection?"

I zoomed in on the woman.

"In case you haven't noticed, I'm not a fleeking doll!"

Diane looked away at her screen. "According to your recent modification stats, your body consists of fifty-two percent cyber enhancements. By the rules of the 2215 Global Cyborg/Human Agreement, you are considered a cyborg and are subject to all conditions pertaining to cyborg repossession."

"Look at me!" I shouted. "I ain't property!"

The woman looked away from the screen again.

"There is a solution," she said. "Your cybernetic parts can be removed. You can then use your severance funds retained by Cytech to regrow those parts released to the collectors."

Of course, that was bullshit. I wouldn't survive the surgery.

"That ain't happening," I said.

Diane gave me a disinterested smile.

"I'm sorry to hear that, Mr. Mejia."

The screen went blank, and my EV shut down. As I descended to the surface, I figured I had about ten minutes before the collectors, or repo knights, showed up. Those muthas were straight A.I., armored from dome to toe and built for carnage. As soon as the EV touched the pavement I was out and running. There was no place I could escape the knights, but there was a place I could go and buy some time while I figured out what the hell to do. I had to dive in the Dumpster.

The Dumpster ain't as much a place as it is a concept. It's an underground reflection of the Net, where you can do anything you want for a helluva lot less. It's how we scrapers survive, how we keep our tech working and our bills paid. The Aytee-EL Dumpster was a few blocks from where I went down; I knew I had reached it before my scan tech crashed. That belonged to Cytech, too. I didn't need it though. I knew exactly where I was going.

The Butcher Shop hid on a backstreet that dead ended on the Beltline. I stood before the door, waiting for the security scan. Two minutes passed and the door didn't open.

"Michelle," I said. "It's me, Carlos."

The door didn't lift.

"Come on, Michelle," I said. "Open the damn door!"

"Fleek off, Carlos," Michelle said. "You're hot."

"No, I'm not!"

"My blockers are working triple time. Leave."

Time was up. I had to move. I was stepping away from the door when the stun round hit me square in the back. Lucky thing my battle tech was on; it dampened the impact, but that shit still hurt. My hand sleeves pulled away as I rolled onto my back, firing a defensive pattern as I tried to stand. The repo knights passed through like a bull through rice paper. The only reason I wasn't dead was that they'd come to collect.

I had no choice. I reached into my back pouch and pulled my Sig Saur. I put two rounds into the first knight's head, three rounds into the other.

"Shield that!" I shouted.

The knights dropped to the ground in a cascade of sparks and fire. The Butcher Shop door lifted and Michelle appeared wearing a dingy work jumper, her hair pulled back and wrapped in a blue scarf. Her brown eyes gazed at me in wonder. Well, not exactly me. My Sig.

"Get inside," she said.

I stumbled into the building, my back sore from the stun round. Michelle smacked her hand against a press button on the interior wall and the door slid shut, her eyes still on my Sig.

"Thanks, I think," I said. I tucked the Sig back into my pack.

"Where did you get that?" she asked.

"None of your business," I replied.

"That's a Sig Saur P940, the last handgun produced by the company before the intergalactic ban on projectile firearms," she said. "It shouldn't exist."

"Yet it does," I replied. "It was a gift from Cytech. They gave me a thousand rounds, too. Never expected me to use it though."

"I want it," Michelle said.

So that was the deal. Whatever I needed her to do was going to cost me my piece.

"I can't just give you this!" I said in mock anger. "It's priceless!"

"Today it has a price," Michelle said. "Your life. I figure those repo knights came to collect your parts, otherwise they would have fried you. I told you not to fleek with Cytech."

"I don't know," I said. "It is valuable."

"It's the only deal you got. Take it or leave it."

I took the Sig from my back holster and handed it over.

"Clips, too."

I feigned despair as I gave her the clips. The truth was that Cytech found a stash of old military gear reclaiming an old nuke site for their latest research facility. They were about to trash it all and I asked if I could take a few things. Sometimes old tech is better than new. I had a roomful of Sigs with enough ammo to last me forever.

Michelle took the Sig and the clips then placed them inside a nearby security cabinet. She finally smiled.

"So, what's your problem?"

"Cytech went under," I said. "And according to the bank I'm an asset to be liquidated."

"I warned you," Michelle replied.

"I don't need to hear that right now," I said. "I need to take some shit out."

"Follow me."

She led me to a room she called the Cutting Board.

"Stand right there," she said, pointing to a bare ceramic circle on the floor. "Hold your arms out."

I assumed the position.

"Scan," she said.

There was a flash of light and a holo appeared beside me, a road map of my insides. Michelle walked up to it, rubbing her chin as she frowned.

"Well?" I said.

Michelle shook her head. "You are so fleeked. Did it ever occur to you to ask what these tech heads were doing to you?"

"No," I confessed. "And if I they told me, I probably wouldn't have understood."

Michelle shook her head. "I don't know what half this shit is. The tech is too new. But I do know one thing; the Bank doesn't want your parts. They want you."

"Shit," I said.

"For real," Michelle replied. "Look at this."

She pointed at my enhancements. "Tech and organics feed on different systems."

"I know that much," I replied.

"But check this out," she continued. "Somehow, they managed to merge your power sources. Your tech can feed off your organics, and your organics can feed off your tech."

"That's why I feel so good in the sun!" I said.

"And why your tech runs longer between charging, I suspect."

13

She was right.

"You're a hybrid," Michelle said. She began pacing.

"This is cutting edge. I don't think Cytech went bankrupt. I think they were shut down. Whoever did this wants this tech, and you're the presentation."

Michelle was right. I was flecked. Big time.

"One more thing," Michelle said.

I rolled my eyes. "What?"

"This."

She pointed at a bright spot glowing near my neck.

"This is your thyroid," she said. "Cytech implanted something to regulate the influence of their implants on your metabolism. Right now, it's dialed down. I think this is what they really want."

"Take it out," I said.

"Not so fast," Michelle replied. "I have an idea why it's there, and the only way to find out for sure is to take it out. But that might kill you."

"Like I have a choice," I replied. "Take it and toss it."

Michelle looked at me like a worried parent.

"Are you sure about this?"

"Take it out and I'll get you a Glock plus enough ammo to last you the rest of your life."

"Let's get you prepped," Michelle said.

Michelle left the room then returned with a chair. "Sit."

I sat in the chair.

"Don't you need to put me to sleep or something?"

Michelle laughed. "You actually thought I was going to operate on you? I cut your throat, and I could sell your carcass to the bank."

"What are you going to do?"

"I'm going to shut it off."

Michelle took something that looked like a small box then placed it against my neck.

"This might hurt," she said.

Hurt was an understatement. When I woke up, I was dizzy and had peed my pants. I jumped out of the chair, which was a mistake. I hit my head on the ceiling then crashed onto the floor. The thing was that Michelle's ceiling was high. Very high. So, there I was lying on the floor with a headache and soiled pants and Michelle looking at me like I had three heads.

"Great gods," she said.

"Why didn't you tell me this was going to hurt?" I said.

"I did. Did you just see how high you jumped?"

I knew what I just did was amazing, but at the moment I just wanted some clean clothes.

"You got a change of clothes around here?" I asked.

"I think so," Michelle answered.

"Where's the shower?" I asked.

Michelle led me to the bathroom. She rustled up a spare pair of pants that fit way too tight but would have to do. I cleaned up the best I could then headed for the door.

"You can't go out there," Michelle said. "Repo knights are probably swarming the district, and you don't know what you're capable of."

"I have an idea," I replied. I could feel it; most of all I could see it. Michelle seemed to be moving in slow motion to me, which meant either my head was fleeked up or my senses were working overtime. Still, she had a point. I wasn't sure if I was ready to face off with a repo swarm.

"Can you ghost me?" I asked.

"It'll cost you," Michelle said.

"How about I throw in a vintage military issue Colt .45?"

Michelle shuffled off to her worktable. In a matter of minutes, she returned with a palm sized drone. She extended her hand then drew it back.

"Wait a minute. How am I going to get all this with your ass on the run?"

I reached into my shirt pocket and handed her my card.

"My codes," I said. "I'm sure you can find out where I live. I'd give it a few weeks to cool down."

"A business card? Really?" she said.

"You can't hack it," I replied.

Michelle took the card and tucked it into her hip pocket.

"What are you going to do now?" she asked.

"Take my chances," I said. "But I have to see someone first."

It wasn't in my nature to run. Well at least not for long. If MWB&T wanted a fight, I'd give it to them. But I would need help.

Michelle went to the door then released the ghost. I was about to step out, but she put her hand on my chest, stopping me.

"Give it a minute."

The drone hovered near the street for a few minutes when a rideshare EV appeared. The door opened, letting out a passenger, and the ghost flew in. The EV lifted into traffic; a minute later three repo knights flew off in pursuit.

"Thanks, Michelle," I said. "I owe you."

"You're paid up in full," Michelle replied. "Good luck. Don't die."

"I don't plan to."

I stepped into the darkness and hurried away. I couldn't trust transport, so I walked. It took me most of the night to cross the city to my destination. The sun was rising as I stepped up to Dedren Carmichael's door. I shook my head looking at the modest home. This man was cheap.

"Carlos, is that you?" Dedren's voice surrounded me.

"You said you needed to see me, and I need your help," I answered.

The door slid open. While Dedren scrimped on the exterior, the inside of his home was immaculate and exquisite. An L6 A.I. greeted me; if it weren't for his purple eyes, I would have thought I was looking at a handsome organic.

"Welcome, Mr. Mejia," it said. "Please follow me to the breakfast area."

I followed the L6. The kitchen was well appointed; Dedren stood over the stove stirring something in a frying pan. He turned to me and smiled.

"Hi Carlos! It's a little early, but I'm glad you're here. Sit. I'm almost done with the eggs."

I sat at the table. The L6 left the room. Dedren sat at the table with a plate of grits, eggs, and bacon. I hadn't eaten in two days, but I wasn't hungry. I guess my hybrid system was running off the battery.

"I know what you're thinking," Dedren said. "A man like me should have more servants. I'm very particular about how I spend my money. Why waste it on something I can do myself?"

Actually, I didn't care, but I did my best to look interested.

"Look, Dedren, I need your help. Cytech went under and now I'm running from the bank trying to save my ass. I need to lay low for a while to work all this out and I figured you can help me."

Dedren scooped up a forkful of grits and ate before answering.

"How do you figure that?" he said with a full mouth.

"I don't know exactly what you do, but I'm sure most of it is dirty," I said. "You help me, and I'll be eternally grateful. And I'll keep my mouth shut about what I do know."

Dedren took a sip of his coffee.

"I'm disappointed, Carlos," he said. "I thought we were friends."

"It's business," I said. "It always is."

Dedren grinned. "True. I must admit though MWS&T moved a lot faster than I expected."

My eyes went wide. "What the fleek are you talking about?"

Dedren ate his eggs before answering me.

"Cytech has always been a pain in my ass," he said. "They were in competition with three of my tech companies, and their latest discovery was rumored to put them out of business. Smart ass bastards. So, I acted first."

"You did this?" I asked. "You?"

Dedren grinned. "I own MWS & T. I called in a few loans and just like that Cytech was broke. We were liquidating their assets and transferring their research to our data hubs when we discovered their work on hybrid cyborgs . . . and you. Do you realize how valuable you are?"

I jumped to my feet to bust a hole in his ass when the house filled with repo knights. Dedren finished his coffee.

"I must admit I didn't expect you to bring the goods to my doorstep. I figured it would take a few weeks to hunt you down. Saved me a lot of time and money."

Battle tech kicked in, moving so fast I could barely keep up. Dedren's eyes went wide.

"Fleek!" he exclaimed just before he dove under the table.

It was like watching a flick, except I was the star. I spun, ducked, dodged, and shot my way through the mob, destroying the interior of Dedren's house in the process. It didn't matter. Once I found out who his partners were, he wouldn't be alive to enjoy it anyway.

I was gunning down the last knight when the L6 tackled me. Had to be a fluke, I thought. There was no way a Pretty Doll could get by my tech. But then I turned to take it out, it hit me with an EMP pulse that shut down my all my tech. I reached for my Sig then cursed; I gave it to Michelle. Last resort was my short machete strapped to my right calf. I snatched it free then lunged for the L6. To my shock it blocked my thrust then kicked me in my chest. I flew across the room then slammed into the wall, my nannies repairing my damaged back as the L6 jumped the gap. I managed to get to my feet as it landed, and it was on. We stood toe to toe, trading kicks and punches. I should have been beating it down, but I wasn't. Dedren must have geeked it from the tech he stole from Cytech. My nannies were falling behind, and I was slowing down. What began as a stalemate became me taking an ass whupping. My legs faltered and I fell, my body rippling with pain. The L6 raised its foot to stomp me when two loud pops echoed in the room. Two holes appeared in the L6's chest area and it fell to the side. When my eyes cleared, I saw Michelle walking toward me with the Sig Saur in her hand. Dedren crawled from under the table and scrambled to his feet. He glared at Michelle.

"Who the fleek are you, bitch?" he shouted.

Michelle turned to him.

"Bitch?"

"Michelle, no!" I said.

Michelle raised the Sig and put two rounds in Dedren's head. She walked to me, a frown on her face.

"What are you doing here?" I said.

She reached into her pocket, pulled out my card then threw it at me. It bounced off my forehead then landed in my lap.

"It didn't work," she said. "I tracked you here to get my guns."

"You put a tracker in me?"

Michelle nodded. "A good thing I did. That L6 was beating you into paste."

She knelt then took out a nano syringe. She stabbed me near my heart, releasing the nannies. I felt better immediately.

"Come on. We need to get out of here."

I stood, feeling better every second. I glanced at Dedren's body. He was behind it all, but there had to be others.

"Come on, Carlos," Michelle said again. "And bring it with you."

She gestured at the L6.

"Why?" I asked.

"Because it was beating your ass, and I want to know why. And because you still owe me."

I shrugged and lifted the L6 onto my shoulders. Together we left the house, climbed into Michelle's repair van then lifted off.

I work for Michelle now. In addition to saving me, she cleaned out Dedren's crypaccount. I was hoping she would break me off a little, but that didn't happen. But I couldn't complain. She pays me more than Cytech, and together we're searching for the others. When we find them, I go after them. I guess you can say I'm Michelle's repo knight now. But I won't be that forever. See, Michelle's not the only smart one. Once I figure out how to control my upgrades, I'm out. Will she be able to find me? Maybe, maybe not. I'm willing to play the odds.

EPISODE TWO:
THE SOURCE

I didn't ask for this. All I wanted was my cut. I could care less how I worked, and long as I worked. I thought hooking up with Michelle was a good idea, but the longer it lasted, the worse it got. But I had to stick around because of the money. We both had enough to live like CEOs anywhere in the UC, but Michelle was being stingy. 'You get yours when we figure this out,' she said. Fleeking hackers. I hate them.

The place we hid out was worse than Michelle's previous haunt. She said we needed to keep a low profile since we took all those cryptos. The rooms were just big enough for a bed and a dresser, which meant as big as I am, I had to practically get naked and oil up so I could slide through the door. So, I spent most of my time in the streets, except when Michelle wanted to tinker with my mech. And she always wanted to tinker with my mech.

That day she'd been fussing with my circuits the entire morning.

"What the hell are you doing?" I finally said.

"Installing the final touches," she replied.

"The final touches of what?"

Michelle looked up from her holoscreen then lifted her glasses until they rested between her afro puffs.

"Why do you want to know?"

"Because I do."

"You never wanted to before."

I folded my arms, almost pulling some of the wires hooked into my ports loose.

"Because nobody ever fucked with me as much as you're doing right now."

"You probably never needed upgrades like you do now," Michelle said.

"Upgrades for what?"

Michelle fell back into her chair then sighed.

"Your tech is way behind the doll we encountered at Dedren's. I need to make sure you're ready."

"Ready for what?"

"Jeez, what's with all the questions? Just trust me, okay?"

I started pulling the cables out. "I don't trust anybody."

Michelle jumped from her chair then grabbed my hand. She's stronger than she looks, but not strong enough. I snatched my hand free and kept pulling.

"Stop Carlos, please?" she said. I was stunned. She said please. Michelle never says please. I stopped pulling the cables free.

"I've learned as much as I can from the doll," she said. "We need to get into Cytech and find out what they have that's so special. In order to do that we need you at top level just in case we run into trouble."

"When we run into trouble," I corrected her. "And what is this we shit?"

"I'm going, too."

"Why? So I can mop you up when one of those gun dolls blasts you into transition?"

"Fleek you," Michelle replied. "I'm not helpless. I got a few tricks up my sleeve."

"Twenty percent," I said.

Michelle blinked. "What?"

"Twenty percent of my take. Today. Otherwise, I'm walking."

23

"Don't you want to know what the earth is going on?"

"Nope," I said. "I want to spend my money and get laid. That's what I want. Unless you give me twenty percent."

Michelle scooted close to the console. Her fingers flew across the holoboard.

"Done."

I tapped my temple. It was there. I took the rest of the cables from my arm and stood.

"Wait!" Michelle yelped. "You said you'd let me finish!"

"I will once I splurge a little. You can have your way with me once I get back."

Fleeking hack bag!" she shouted as I opened the door.

"Back at you, meat bag hag."

"What did you call me?"

That's when I heard the pop of an EMP, and everything went rigid. I swayed then fell forward. I managed to turn my head before I crashed into the floor, saving my nose from being broken. My jaw wasn't as fortunate. I heard Michelle walk up to me. She hooked the cables back into my arms and legs.

"I tried to be nice," she said. "Look what you made me do."

"Just get it over with," I mumbled.

"You'll thank me later, I promise."

"We'll see," I replied.

I laid on the floor while Michelle did her thing. I decided we were going to have to have a long talk after this was done. Organics forget that we have feelings, too. We can't . . . well we shouldn't be cut off and on when they feel like it. Show some respect goddammit.

Although I was pissed, I had to admit whatever she was doing felt pretty good. It was like I was growing inside, like things were coming closer together. The best way to describe it was like falling in love with yourself. I know that sounds freaky, but hey; I'm not a poet.

"There," she said. "Upgrade complete."

She crawled over me, unhooking the wires.

"You can stand up now."

I took my time rising. The last time Michelle upgraded me I almost popped through the roof. I worked my arms and did a few squats. The lag I usually experienced between thought and action was completely gone.

"Fleek!" I said. "What did you do?"

"Dedren's doll had significant synaptic density improvements," she said. "I did the same to you. I also increased your A.I. muscle density by thirty-five percent. You're strong as shit now. Finally, I increased your nano capacity by ten percent. You're welcome."

"Excellent." I strode for the door. "I'll be back in a few days."

Michelle didn't answer. I reached for the door pad, expecting her to yell at me or something. She didn't.

"You're not going to try to stop me?" I asked.

"Nope."

I turned to see her smiling.

"Go do what you need to do," she said. "It'll give you a chance to get used to the upgrades. Just promise me you won't kill anybody while you're gone. We don't need the extra attention."

"I can't promise you that," I said. "I will promise that I won't leave any evidence."

"Fair enough," Michelle said. "When you get back, I'll be ready."

Those last words made me nervous.

"Ready for what?"

"You'll see. Now go. I got work to do."

I pressed my hand against the door pad. The door swished open and the cool Aytee-El wind flowed around me. It felt invigorating.

"See you in a few," I said.

I stepped outside and smiled as I heard the door close behind me. My attention was immediately captured by the nightlights and buzz of ground and aerial traffic. It was going to be a helluva three days.

* * *

Four days later I strolled down the street with a big ass smile on my face. Magic City was everything they said and some. I didn't have time to find an organic with a cyborg fetish or a fellow metal, so I went straight for the paid entertainment. Every crypto was well spent. Best of all, I didn't kill anybody. There was this one meat bag who decided he wanted to show everyone how strong he was by challenging me to a fight. A crazy foot-baller. I took it easy on him and choked him out. Never let it be said that I'm not a kind person.

I pressed my hand on the pad and the door swished open. I expected to see Michelle waiting with her arms folded and tapping her foot. I knew she was tracking me; she probably had cameras on me, too. The thought made me hesitate; was she watching me the entire time? That would be freaky, but probably entertaining, too. I shrugged; I wasn't the shy type, and if she did have footage, I could sell it on the gray market. Use some of her techie stuff to alter the faces and just like that I'd have a new revenue stream. Something to consider at least.

"Michelle!" I called out. "I'm back. Where the fleek are you?"

I was answered by a bolt that hit me square in my chest, knocking me through the door and back out into the street. Battle tech popped up, sharing my vitals and target perspectives. Fifteen per cent damage and I felt every bit of it. I rolled to my right and the concrete where I was exploded. My leg lifted and a pulse bolt fired from my heel. When Michelle installed that, I don't know, but I thanked her ass for it. The shot gave me time to regain my feet and assess the situation.

A fully armored battleborg charged out of the building, blasters blazing. My enhanced shielding deflected the barrage, and I ran toward it. Normally I would have preferred a firefight, but I was pissed. The thing was still shooting point blank when I pivoted on my right foot and punched it in the faceplate. The borg staggered back and I kicked it in the chest plate then swept it off its feet. I jumped on top of it, pounding it with my fists until I was covered with metal parts and lubricant. There was a hissing then the cyborg went limp.

I climbed off the metal head then searched for Michelle, or what was left of her.

"Michelle! Michelle!"

I was answered by a clanging sound. I followed it until I stood before a large metal door at the back of the building. At least she made it to the saferoom. My worry faded and I tapped on the door.

"Michelle, you in there?"

"Yes!" she yelled. "Let me out!"

"I forgot how to," I replied.

"Quit fleeking with me and let me out!"

I punched in the code then turned the crank. The door opened and Michelle spilled out drenched with sweat.

"I need to put a ventilation system in there," she said between gasps.

"I'm okay," I said. "Thanks for asking. What the hell was that and why was it here?"

Michelle sat up and pulled at her afro puffs.

"I fleeked up," she said. "When I duplicated the code from Dedren's doll I must have set off a homing code. They tracked us here then sent that battle bot to finish us off. Which means we gotta get the fleek out of here fast."

We ran through the building grabbing armfuls of shit and tossing it into the EV. We jumped inside and Michelle took out something that looked like a giant controller.

"What are you going to do with that?" I asked.

"Drive," Michelle answered.

"You hack the traffic grid and the APD will be on us like flies on shit."

"As far as they know, we are APD," Michelle replied with a grin.

Michelle worked the EV through the congested traffic, dipping from air to ground and back again.

"Where we going?" I finally asked. "A new hideout?"

"Sort of," she replied. "We're going to Beijing."

Michelle drove us to Jackson/Hartfield. She parked the car in the economy deck then tagged it with an ID scrambler. That would keep the lot droids occupied for at least two weeks. I followed her to the conveyer which sped us to the terminal. As we walked to the gate, she swiped her forearm in my direction. My screen appeared; we were flying first class non-stop. A little red light flashed in the corner of my eye, and I grinned. Michelle had us prescreened. She knew there was no way I could get through any kind of security with all the gear I packed. Neither would she. We were quiet until we reached our section. We both fell into our seats and ordered drinks. I was on my third vodka before Michelle cleared her throat.

"What?"

"Aren't you going to ask me why we're going to Beijing?"

I downed a fourth drink.

"No."

Michelle slumped into her lounger. "I don't get you. One minute you're bitching about modifications and now you don't give a flit about where we're headed?"

I sighed. "Okay. Where are we going?"

Michelle grinned. "You ever heard of Jiadan Prosthetics?"

"Sure," I said. "They make doll parts."

"They made your legs and arms," Michelle said.

"Really? Cool." I downed another vodka. Michelle took the bottle from me before I could make another drink.

"Why are you drinking so much?"

"Because I hate flying," I said.

"You can fly, in case you haven't noticed."

I was stunned. She never tells me anything.

"Anyway, it seems that the chair, Liu Jiaying, was a business partner of Dedren's. There's no direct link between them, but they worked with each other through various shell companies. I think she was responsible for limb creation. Dedren was financing the entire operation as well as in charge of intellectual acquisition. That's why he shut down your patrons; to acquire their doll tech."

Our jet began rolling and I became dizzy. I strapped in.

"Here we go," I whispered.

Michelle grimaced. "You're not going to throw up, are you?"

My stomach growled.

"It depends on how long the flight is," I said.

"We can't have that," Michelle replied.

I got a bad feeling.

"Michelle, wait…"

* * *

When I woke up, we were landing in Beijing. Michelle yawned, stretched then shared a sweet smile. Apparently, she went to sleep, too, except in her case it was voluntarily.

"You have to stop doing that shit," I said.

"It was for your own good," she replied. "And mine. The last thing I wanted to see was you throwing up."

The jet taxied to the gate, and we exited. My translator switched automatically as we hurried down the tunnel to the airport exit. Michelle summoned a Rick, and we were on our way.

"What's the plan?" I asked.

"We need to talk to Jiaying," Michelle said. "I've been through her files a million times, and I can't find the final contact. There's only one place she could be keeping it where I can't find it."

"Where is that?" I asked.

Michelle tapped her head.

"Her memory?"

"Yep. I figure she, Dedren and the unknown partner communicated verbally when it came to the real important shit."

"So, we just going to walk up to her, ask her what's going on and she's going to tell us everything?"

"Of course not," Michelle replied. "We're going to interview her."

I nodded. Interview must be Michelle's nice way of saying kidnap and interrogate. I'd been involved in a few kidnappings. Usually, it was some startup company biting off too much of the profit pie. I'd knock them out, take them somewhere deserted, then convince them to sell their company before they ended up like me. One thing about company types; they don't handle pain too well.

"Sounds like a plan."

Michelle looked at me for a moment before a shocked look took over her face.

"Oh gods, no, not like that," she said.

I was confused. "How else is she going to tell us what we want to know?"

"Don't worry about that," Michelle said. "I'll handle it. Here's the hard part. She lives in her work building and the security is pretty tight. If things go to flit, we might have to fight our way out."

"Give me the building plans," I said.

Michelle swiped the plans to me. I broadcasted a holo then studied the schematics. I integrated my battle tech, looking for ambush points and escape scenarios.

"Got it," I said.

"Now give it to me," Michelle said.

"Why? I got it."

"Just in case we get separated."

"If we get separated, nice knowing you."

Michelle rolled her eyes. "Send me the fleeking schematics."

I swiped them to her. She did a quick check then nodded.

"C'mon. We need new clothes. Tailor," she said.

The Rick took us to Beijing's garment district. Apparently, the people of Beijing liked to shop outside, unlike the folks in Aytee-El. The Rick flew to a shop at the end of a narrow, crowded alley then landed in front its bare walls. A person stepped through the door, greeting us with a warm smile and a bow. I did a quick scan; it was 100% doll.

"Welcome to Ming's" it said in English. "How can I assist you?"

Michelle bowed. "We need formal business clothing."

The doll returned her bow then gestured to the entrance.

"Please follow me."

It led us into the shop. It was sparse, a decent scanner and printer the only items inside. The doll guided Michelle to the scanner.

"Please remain still during measuring," it said.

Michelle did as she was told. The doll activated the scanner and Michelle was doused with a blue grid. Moments later the printer was activated. Michelle stepped out of the scanner and the doll looked at me then gestured. I entered and the scanner did its thing. The printer had completed Michelle's wardrobe by the time I stepped out.

"The dressing room is in the rear of the shop," the doll said.

Michelle disappeared to change clothes while I waited for my outfit. The synth-tailor stared at me with a blank expression. Whoever owned it was too cheap to pay for proper emotion codes. It blinked when printing was complete and remove my outfit. I took it and headed to the dressing room. I met Michelle on the way. She sported a loose-fitting navy-blue pantsuit that easily covered her body armor.

"You clean up good," I said.

"Thank you. Now get dressed. We don't want to be late for our appointment."

The dressing room was cramped, of course. I managed to wiggle into my outfit despite that and was impressed. The tailor mech was accurate for a piece of junk. When I returned to the room Michelle's eyebrows rose.

"You actually look good," she said.

"You seemed surprised," I replied.

"I am. Now let's go."

Michelle transferred the payment to the doll, and we were on our way. She fiddled with her wrist console then swiped me the data.

"Netview credentials," I said. "Nice. I always wanted to be on the net."

"Don't get used to it," Michelle replied. "I gave us a sixty-minute firewall."

"Is that enough time?"

"It better be."

Ten minutes later we arrived at Jiadan Prosthetics. To say the sprawling office and manufacturing facility was huge would be a lie. It was a city within itself, occupying six klicks of land.

"Somebody's paying a helluva lot of tax cryptos," I said.

"You can afford it when you make all your workers," Michelle replied.

The Rick pulled up to the entrance then rolled to a stop as the security cams scanned us.

"Here we go," Michelle said.

The cams lifted and the gate slid open. I did a quick check of my systems to make sure Jiadan security didn't disable anything. When I was done, I gave Michelle a wink.

"You're good," I said.

"You haven't figured that out yet?" she replied.

"Makes me wonder about you being a junk jockey. What did you do before?"

"A lot of stuff," Michelle replied. "Nothing worth mentioning."

"So how did you learn all this?"

Michelle shrugged. "You'll be surprised what people leaving laying around when they underestimate the help. I'm naturally curious."

"Which means you steal a lot of shit."

"Something like that," Michelle replied. "Never thought I'd get to use most of it until you came along."

The Rick jerked still then resumed its course.

"Do not be alarmed," a pleasant voice spoke. "For your convenience we have assumed guidance of your transportation. You will be taken directly to your destination. Thank you for visiting Jiadan Prosthetics."

I got a worry bubble in my gut and looked at Michelle.

"We're okay. Trust me," she said.

I don't trust anybody.

The Rick stopped in front of a one-story building located in the center of the complex. Meat bags walked in and out, the only ones we'd seen since entering the complex. Apparently, Ms. Liu didn't trust the dolls with the important stuff. She must know people like Michelle. I laughed at the thought.

"What are you laughing about?" Michelle asked.

"Nothing," I replied, then laughed again.

"Remind me to check you out when we get back."

"If we get back," I said then winked.

A receptionist met us as soon as we entered the building. The tall woman wore a tight-fitting jumpsuit with the Jiadan logo on the left breast. She smiled and bowed.

"Welcome to Jiadan," she said. "I am Yu Yan, Ms. Liu's assistant. She asked me to take you to the conference room. She'll meet with you momentarily."

"Thank you," Michelle replied. "We appreciate her seeing with us on such short notice."

"We are honored," Yu Yan replied. "It's not often the media shows an interest in businesses like ours. We provide a necessary service, but what we do is not sexy."

"That depends on if you're a doll or a meat bag," I said.

Yu Yan gave me a scolding look.

"We do not allow such language on our premises, Mr....?"

"Smith," Michelle said. "John Smith. I'm Jane Doe."

I glared at Michelle. She rolled her eyes.

"I apologize," I said. "My assignments usually deal with the darker side of our society."

"You are forgiven," Yu Yan said with a smile. "Now if you will please follow me, Ms. Liu is waiting."

We followed Yu Yan down the long corridor to the CEO's suite. Yu Yan opened the door, revealing Ms. Liu sitting at her desk. She was a stunning woman, tall, with long black hair and an engaging smile. She stood then gestured to the chairs in front of her desk.

"Miss Doe, Mr. Smith. Welcome to Jiadan. Please sit down."

I followed Michelle to the chairs, and we sat.

"So, I think we should begin by being honest with each other," Michelle said. "My name is not Jane Doe, and his name is not John Smith. I'm Michelle Carter, and this is my friend, Carlos Mejia."

It took everything in my power to keep from punching Michelle in the side of the head. She gave me up! Ms. Liu's eyes narrowed as she studied me, then she looked at Michelle and laughed.

"That was obvious. I guess now you expect me to be honest."

Michelle smiled. "Of course."

"What do you wish to know?" she asked.

Michelle leaned forward. "What does this manufacturing facility really do?"

"We make cybernetic limbs," Ms. Liu said. "As a matter of fact, we made Mr. Mejia's limbs, if I'm correct."

"I don't think so," I said. "I got these bad boys in Windy City."

"They may have been installed there, but I'm certain they are Jiadan made. Ninety-eight percent of all prosthetics are made by us or our affiliates."

"What about other parts?" Michelle asked. "Torsos, skulls, brains, organs…"

"I know what you're seeking, Ms. Carter, but you won't find it here," Ms. Liu said. "UC regulations forbid the manufacture of pure symbiots. We are many things at Jiadan, but we are not lawbreakers."

Ms. Liu stood, indicating the interview was over.

"I must say, I'm impressed by your boldness," she said. "Most scandal casts try to hack us. You walked right through the door. I'd love to take you on a tour of our facility to prove to you that we're quite legitimate."

"Why would you do that?" Michelle asked. "You could have thrown us out at any minute."

"I could have," she said. "But you amuse me, and Mr. Mejia is quite interesting."

"It seems we're out of time," Michelle said. "Another day, perhaps?"

"Of course," Ms. Liu said. "I look forward to it."

Ms. Liu led us to the door.

"Yu Yan will see you out. It's been interesting."

Yu Yan appeared moments later. We followed her to the exit; our Rick waiting for us.

"What was that all about?" I said. "I thought we were going to be discreet."

"I changed my mind," Michelle said. "Besides, I learned everything I needed to know."

As we entered the Rick a tiny object flew inside then landed in Michelle's palm. She looked at it then grinned. My eyes went wide.

"That's a Tacdrone," I said. "Hi-security shit. What the fleek are you doing with that?"

"I work the gray market," Michelle replied. "How do you think I got it?"

The Rick lifted then cruised for the gate.

"So, we were just shooting the shit while little bit did all the hard work?"

"No," Michelle replied. "I wanted to force her hand. I figured if I suggested that we knew what she was doing and I dangled you in her face, she would act."

"But she didn't," I said.

"Not . . ."

The Rick jolted then spun, knocking us around like a blender. I did my best not to crash into Michelle, but her squealing let me know that I failed. Battle tech kicked in; we'd been hit by an EMP. The Rick crashed and we were enveloped by shock suppressers. I kicked the door open then pulled Michelle free. I thought she would be injured. Instead, she was pissed.

"That bitch!" she screamed.

"I thought you didn't like that word," I said.

"Only when someone calls me one," she replied. "For her it fits."

My battle tech went into high gear. Thirty security thugs were coming fast. We were only a half a klick from the gate; if we could get into the street the thugs would have to back off. Michelle had already figured that out; she was halfway to the gate before I started running. With my enhanced legs I caught up with her in seconds. Luckily for us there was no one stationed at the gate. I lowered my shoulder and powered through. The metal barrier hit the street, skidding into traffic, and causing a mess. We took a sharp left then ran down the down the middle of the road in between lifts.

"This was a bad idea," I said.

"You didn't have a better one," Michelle replied.

"Yes, I did. You didn't ask."

A bolt struck my shoulder, knocking me off balance. I caught myself then spun about. The Jiadan security jocks decided the rules weren't shit. They were coming for us. I grabbed Michelle then threw her up on my shoulders. I ran full out, streaking by EVs that swerved to avoid hitting me.

"I told you this was a bad idea!" I shouted.

"Shut up and run faster!" Michelle shouted back.

I was about to throw her into a dumpster when a shadow passed over us. I stopped and skidded to a halt, holding onto Michelle to keep her from flying off my shoulders. Something landed a few feet in front of us, breaking the asphalt and showering us with dust. When it cleared, my heart dropped.

"Oh shit," Michelle whispered.

"Tell me about it," I replied.

The A.I. stood about my height. It was fully armored with a head bristling with video and audio sensors. It crouched then extended its right arm. A laser blade emerged.

"It's got a sword," I said. "A fleeking sword!"

"You have one, too," Michelle replied.

I look at her with a grimace.

"Since when?"

"Since I put one in you."

I summoned my guns and fired in automatic mode. That damn A.I. blocked almost every shot with that sword. What it didn't block its shields absorbed.

"That's not going to work," Michelle said. "Let me handle this."

"What the fleek are you…"

She swiped her forearm and a holo controller appeared before her. Suddenly I couldn't feel my arms and legs.

"Michelle, what's happening?"

The A.I. rose from the pavement then streaked for us. I was helpless; or at least I thought I was. My guns receded. A long beam materialized from my right hand; an elliptical energy shield formed at the end of my left arm.

"What the fleek?"

My shield lifted and blocked the A.I.'s swing. I countered with my sword and the fight was on. Except I wasn't fighting. Michelle was. And she was doing a damn good job. She and the A.I stood toe to toe matching blow for blow. The problem was a small army of security thugs were closing in on us and this fight was about to become uneven.

"Give me my legs!" I said.

"No!" Michelle replied.

"Give me my legs, dammit!" I yelled. "I can end this!"

"Fine!" Michelle said.

Sensation return to my legs. This time when the A.I. stabbed at us I pivoted to my right. The A.I. adjusted, swinging at my chest. I jumped back then shuffled to my left.

"Excellent!" Michelle shouted.

With some of my body control back my battle tech reactivated, giving me an analysis of the A.I. A pattern of red flashing lights indicated stress points and vulnerable spots.

"Go for the neck!" I said to Michelle. "That's the weak spot!"

"Check!" Michelle yelled.

I danced and Michelle fought. Each blow to the neck weakened the juncture. A meat bag would have picked up on the strategy and altered their defense, but this was an A.I. playing out logical patterns and focused on taking us out. After slipping another sword thrust, I jumped at the A.I.

"Now!" I shouted.

Michelle knocked the A.I. sword aside with the shield then hit the sweet spot. Its head dislodged, hit the street then skidded into a food cart.

There was no time to celebrate; a bolt hit me square in the back, knocking me face first into the street. Michelle managed to jump free then shoulder rolled to her feet. How the hell did she do that?

I clambered to my feet then pivoted about. My nose was broken, but I didn't have time for that. Two large battle sleds had joined the security troops. Where Jaidan got them, I had no I idea. Ms. Liu was sitting there lying her ass off big time.

I grabbed Michelle's arm and pushed her behind me just before the shooting started. My shields took the brunt, Battle tech decreased about 35% before recharging.

"We got to get out of here!" I said.

"No," Michelle replied. "We stay here until I've seen it all."

"All of what?"

"Everything they got."

I was getting pissed at her hard-headed ass.

"I can't go on the offense," I said. "It's taking all I have to protect us. We got to jack!"

"You handle the sleds," she said. "I'll handle the goons."

"With what?"

Michelle answered by jumping out my shield and sprinting at the guards. She slammed into a group of them, arms and legs punching and kicking. By the time they realized what was going on she had a blaster rifle in her hand and was gunning them down. I added my fire-power to hers and the guards scattered for cover. But the sleds kept coming.

I took another direct blast from one of the sleds before beginning evasive movements. Shields were down 45% and coming up slower than before. I could feel the nanos working overtime, my body hot from their activity. I dodged a bolt from the second sled then jumped, soaring the final thirty meters between us and landing on the closest sled. I gripped the hatch with my left hand, ripped it open then jammed my right arm in and lit it up. Wrong move. The sled exploded and sent me airborne. I crashed into a nearby building then slid down the wall onto the pavement.

Battle tech flickered then steadied. Shield down 66%. I looked up to see the other battle sled cruising my way. I looked for Michelle; she was pinned down behind a concrete wall, the security team creeping closer. I couldn't take another direct hit, at least not yet, but I couldn't leave Michelle pinched. So, I lay there, hoping my timing would be perfect.

"One...two...three!"

The battle sled fired. I rolled; the blast missed, gouging the wall. I targeted the security guards then sprayed them, taking out five and sending the rest fleeing for cover. Michelle gave me thumbs up then popped over the barricade, taking down three more guards before they could hide. That woman was good; as a matter of fact, she was too good.

I jumped to my feet then ran, using the Mech to keep from getting shot. But then I zigged when I should have zagged, and a bolt hit me square in the back. The world went black; when my vision returned, I was look-ing at the pavement and a fuzzy battle tech screen. Shields were down 75% and decreasing; vitals were slip-ping faster than my nanos could repair. It's one thing to know you're dying, but it's another thing to watch the stats. Someone grabbed me then flipped me on my back; it was Michelle.

"Hang in there, doll boy," she said. "Back up is coming."

A squadron of UCS EVs passed overhead then explosions shook the pavement.

"Back up?" I croaked. "Who the fleek is back…"

My screen flatlined, and so did I.

* * *

The room was sanitary white like a hospital, but it wasn't. I lay on a slab of steel that chilled my back and my ass. I was plugged in all over, some comfortable, some not, some that felt kinda good. Somebody saved my life. Whether it was good or bad, I'd find out soon.

The wall swished opened and Michelle strolled in with a big smile on her face. I was shocked, not by who she was, but what she wore; a snug fitted dark green UCS uniform, with captain bars on her collar. Everything fell into place.

"How you are feeling, doll boy?" she asked.

"Pretty good for someone about to do time," I replied. "Fleek! Is Michelle actually your name?"

"Yes," Michelle said. "I'm not good with fake first names. And you're not under arrest."

I blinked and my Battle tech appeared. I was 75% healed. Whatever else needed fixing, my nanos could handle it. I began unhooking the cables.

"Be careful," Michelle warned. "You were pretty much done in."

"I don't know if I should be thanking you, based on where I've ended up."

"You should. We cut it close. Jaidan was hiding a lot more than we bargained for. Took us three days to secure the premises."

I looked a little closer. I was butt-ass naked. I couldn't wait to see the gifs. Michelle didn't seem fazed by it. Until a few minutes ago I was evidence.

"So, what happens now?" I asked. "You take all my tech and send me back into the world a meat bag?"

"You never really understood how valuable you are," Michelle replied.

"I told you I didn't care about that stuff. As long as I can kick ass and get laid, I'm good."

Michelle pulled up a chair. She turned it backwards then sat, resting her arms on the backrest.

"You're a prototype," she said. "The mega-corporations were evaluating A.I. tech in you and other hybrids. They couldn't do it as full A.I. because of UC codes, so they separated the tech. You were limbs; there were others for torso, cranial and internals. All the data went to Jaidan for evaluation and implementation."

"Mega-corporations? I thought they were banned."

"They are, officially," Michelle said. But people always find a way around the rules. Usually when we discover them, we tax their shoes off. The system must be maintained. Nobody's rich, but nobody's starving. Plus, we all know how it turns out when corporations run the show. We have a nearly dead planet to remind us."

"So, I was the key," I said.

"Sure were. The day you came running to my shop was the day the lid blew off. I'd been sitting in that shithole for years looking for evidence, then here you come all desperate and loaded with illegal tech. The corporations are trying to build an army, an A.I. army. They mean to take things back to the way it used to be just when we've got the planet healing. We're not going to let that happen."

All this war talk was over my head. I had more personal concerns.

"Since I delivered the goods, I figure I should be paid," I said.

Michelle handed me a vidchip. On the screen was my share of Dedren's cryptos…and hers. I was about to put it in my pocket until I remembered I didn't have on pants.

"What's next? You make me work for the UCS?"

Michelle shook her head.

"You've done more than enough. Once you're 100% you can get dressed and go."

"And I get to keep my tech?"

Michelle nodded. "Just don't take any corporate jobs for the next twenty years. But with the cryptos you have, you won't need to."

The door swished open again and an officer walked in with a rack of clothes. Michelle stood and took an eyeful.

"I'm going to give you some privacy," she said.

She and the other officer left the room. I reattached the cables and let myself heal to 100% as I considered my future. I was richer than anyone with my attitude had a right to be. Knowing me, I'd be broke in a year. If I disciplined myself, I could probably make it two.

Two hours later I was dressed and ambling through the UCS office. I reached the exit and grinned. We were in Aytee-El. If I was going to blow some cryptos, Aytee-El was the perfect place to start.

"Don't be a stranger," Michelle said. "And keep in touch."

I laughed as I turned to see her leaning against the wall, her arms folded.

"Something tells me you'll always know where I am."

Michelle laughed. "I got to protect my investment."

A thought crossed my mind and I decided to follow it.

"You should come with me," I said. "We make a good team."

"Nah," she replied. "I got a good man at home that hasn't seen me in a year. I can't wait to get reacquainted. Besides, it's war time, remember?"

"For you maybe," I said.

I opened the door to walk out.

"Be careful, Carlos," Michelle said. "Jaidan was just the tip of the iceberg."

'I'll try," I replied. "But you know me."

"Right," Michelle replied. "Always playing the odds."

I winked. "You know it."

I stepped out onto the pavement and summoned a Rideout. It was spring in Aytee-El; the dogwoods were in bloom and the smell of flowers in the air. I looked back into UCS headquarters. Michelle still stood there with a smile on her face. I waved, she waved back, then I climbed into the Rideout, ready to start my life over again one more time.

EPISODE THREE: TURNAROUND

They were on me as soon as I stepped out of the café. They'd been following me all day, so I led them on a merry chase. Aytee-EL was my stomping grounds, and I knew every nook and cranny despite the fact I hadn't set foot in the city in over three years. Some things never change, but then some things do.

Three years ago, I was Michelle Carter, high ranking intelligence officer for UCS (United Cities Security). After bringing down the illegal A.I. operation at Jaidan, I was on the fast track to a division manager position. I'd given up a normal utopian life and a marriage to help protect what the Hackers had built. Now I was on the run, considered a traitor to the very system I used to protect by the people who I was defending the system from. It was kaka, and I was mad as fleek.

My pursuers follow me into a narrow alley which led to The Dump. I knew as soon as they stepped into the corridor their tech would be screwed. So would mine, but I didn't need it. I was 85% organic, but they were 100% A.I. Three years ago, they would have been illegal. Now they were hunting me down 'for the safety of the System.' The System was about to become a little more unsafe by three.

I ducked behind a battered dumpster, pulled out my loaded Sig Saur then waited. My wrist scanner indicated the dolls were standing at the edge of the alleyway but were not entering. I figured they updated their profiles since the last encounter with me and were being cautious. Moments later my suspicions were confirmed when my scanner picked up the dolls releasing a drone swarm. The swarm sought electronic and infrared spoor. I was good on the electronic front, but my body heat would give me away. I pushed the button in the palm of my left hand, activating my cold suit, dropping my exterior temperature to mirror the dumpster. All I had to do was stay perfectly still and the drones would pass right by.

But then a damn cat sprang from the dumpster, and I yelped. A barrage of pulse fire slammed into the dumpster, almost pushing it over me. I shuffled to keep pace with it, hoping the A.I.s would cease fire since they had no visual confirmation I was behind the trash bin. But they kept shooting.

I dashed from behind the disintegrating block of metal and returned fire. Two hunters went down; I could have taken out the third if I hadn't run out of ammo. I managed to jump behind a nearby corner before it began shooting again as it pursued me. I didn't run; I lay flat on the ground while I reloaded. As the hunter made the turn around the corner, I shot high, shattering its head unit. The hunter went limp then fell on top of me, knocking the wind out of me. Once I caught my breath, I shoved it away, clambered to my feet and took off. I had to put as much distance between me and the alley as possible before the backup units arrived.

As I moved deeper into The Dump, despair set in. I reached into my pocket, took out a Bright and tossed it into my mouth. I gave up on mental motivation a long time ago. Brights kept me sane, although the crash a few hours later would have me balled up like a baby and crying my eyes dry.

I emerged from the alley and into the heart of The Dump. I stopped to get my bearings. Nothing had changed much; the streets bustled with ATLiens going about their day, the skies filled with traffic. I relaxed a little but not completely. The hunters would have a harder time finding me here because just about everyone in the Dump had something to hide. They would have to resort to good old-fashioned physical i.d., and I was an expert at avoiding that. I tucked my weapons away then strolled into the open. I needed a place to rest, and I knew just where to go.

The chamber hostel was a few blocks from the alley. A group of people hung about the entrance, which was normal. I worked my way through them to the clerk, an old model A.I. with a puppet face and a rigid grin.

"Welcome to . . ."

I cut it off by placing my hand on the pass counter. The chits were taken from my account and the passcode uploaded to my band. The chamber number appeared on my screen, and I made my way down the wide hall to my sector. The door flashed green as I neared. I rolled my eyes. It was a bed chamber. I was hoping for a room so I could at least sit at a table, but that wasn't going to be. I climbed into the chamber then closed and secured the door. At least it had enough room for me to sit up. I pulled up my holo-comp then viewed my case. Yes, I kept a case on myself. Force of habit. I looked at every encounter I had since going into hiding. What I expected was true, which made me sad. The time between encounters was decreasing. Every time they found me; they got a little bit better at finding me again. Despite all my experience they were building a profile of me which helped them predict my next move. I shut off the holo-monitor then collapsed on my bed. It was inevitable they were going to catch me.

It began four years ago. Our office personnel disappeared in the first sweep. Low level agents held out a little longer but were rounded up in a few months. Which left the experienced folks like me, and we took the hint. We scattered, knowing it was easier for us to hide alone than hide together. I had no idea if the others were still on the run or had been captured. For all I knew, I was the only one left.

I sat up and turned my holo-comp back on and began searching for someone.

"Come on," I whispered. "I know you're out there somewhere."

I was looking for Carlos Mejia. The truth was that even if I were to find my work colleagues, I wouldn't be sure if they were still on the run or had been turned. But I knew Carlos. If he was still doing what he had been doing, he'd be available to the highest bidder. Plus, we had a history. The problem was it was as if he never existed. I could find no trace of him on the Mesh. He apparently paid a high-class hacker to wipe his existence clean. I couldn't blame him; our adventures had put him on a lot of shit lists. At least I knew what he did with some of the money I let him walk away with. He owed me for that reason alone. If only I could find him.

I finally forced myself to sleep. Gods knows I needed it. When I woke, I was rested but hungry. I thought about having something delivered, but I needed some fresh air. I also needed new clothes. I climbed out of my chamber and headed to the streets. Dusk had settled over the city, the streetlights activating as I exited the hostel. I punched my GIP for the closest ramen joint; it had a bunch of five star reviews, so I set out for it. As I strolled down the street darkness settled a little sooner than I expected. I noticed people looking up. I did the same and discovered the reason for the sudden darkness. The floating cities had returned, and one was passing over The Dump. I sneered at it; the hovering metropolises were the ultimate sign of Elite decadence, serving no purpose other than a playground for the grossly rich. The fact that they existed again meant we were only a few stupid decisions from losing Utopia.

I was about to shake a fist at it until an idea popped into my head.

"Could he be?" I asked aloud.

I shook my head. No, not Carlos. It was highly likely that the people who wanted him dead resided in those soaring monstrosities. If he showed his face, he'd be captured, disassembled, and dissected before he could yell fleek. And yet . . .

I lost my appetite. I would eat later. For the moment, I had to figure out how to get on one of those floating cities.

I locked my GIP on the city then stopped at the ramen joint. It was hard keeping my eyes focused on my meal even though I knew my GIP kept track. I ate as fast as I could without looking hurried then lifted my bowl, drinking the remaining broth before leaving the restaurant and following my GIP.

I was playing a hunch. Though the floaters were supposed to be self-sustaining, the truth was that they had to resupply. Since this one was hovering lower than normal, I suspected it was about to do just that. I ambled through Aytee-El, following the city out of the Dump. I amped my surveillance, keeping my head low and my eyes lowered. The city finally slowed then halted over an industrial sector. It probably needed to recharge its engines in addition to resupplying. I strode to the area, hoping I wouldn't be noticed. As I neared my suspicions were confirmed. Hidden under the city's shadow was a huge refueling station.

There were no gates, so I walked onto the grounds, my mind racing on how I was going to get up there without being noticed. I viewed the various supply vehicles and found what I was looking for, the commissary lift. I decided I didn't have time to play games. I'd be direct, and if that didn't work, I'd shoot somebody.

The city was anchored, its bay doors open. Drone shuttles lifted and descended like metal bees, loading and unloading cargo. An inventory tech stood nearby, watching the process. Low grade A.I.s handled the cargo on ground, organizing the gear for disposal or recycling. They were illegal, but no one cared when it came to keeping the elite living at the level they were accustomed to. I made sure my guns were loaded and my bolter fully charged before strolling up to the tech and tapping their shoulder.

The tech spun in my direction; face obscured by a black screen filled with constantly changing numbers.

"Who are you and what do you want?" the tech asked.

"The first question doesn't matter," I replied. "The second I'll answer. I need to get up there and I need your help."

I gestured to the city. The tech tapped the side of their helmet, and everything ceased. They tapped another button, revealing a umber woman with an angry expression.

"You got six seconds before I call security," she said.

"Check your crypto account, Kecia," I replied.

"How do you know my . . ."

"Don't worry about it. Just check your account."

Kecia dropped her shield screen. A code stream flashed across it then she lifted it, her eyes wide.

"Who the fleek are you?" she said.

"It doesn't matter," I replied. "Get me up there and you'll never see me again."

"I don't want no trouble," Kecia said.

"You already got it if you accepted my transfer."

"Shit!" Kecia said. She scanned the area before speaking again.

"I have to go up to confirm inventory. You go with me. If anybody asks who you are, tell them you're CHI inspection."

"I have a feeling you've done this before," I said.

"Pretties always looking to get Up Top," Kecia replied. "They think those damn high lifers are going to fall in love and keep them around. The lucky ones end up there."

Kecia nodded her head toward the trash bins. My forehead got hot, and I gritted my teeth. A lot of people fought and died to keep shit like this from happening, and here it was again.

"What do I do?" I asked.

"Stay beside me," Kecia said. "Loading will be done in a sec. We'll catch a lift then."

"Don't fleek with me," I said.

"I like living," Kecia replied. Don't worry about me. You, on the other hand, are crazy."

I stood beside Kecia trying to look official as she completed her task. Kecia was Dumpster; I sensed it by the way she agreed so easily to help me. Dump divers know the score. Take the pay and keep your mouth shut.

The last drone descended from the city. A few seconds later a personal rolled up then stopped in front us.

"Hop in," Kecia said.

I climbed into the vehicle, and we ascended to the city cargo hold. It was a quick ride up. We entered a massive cargo bay, bustling with driverless vehicles and plain jane sorters. The vehicle landed and I exited.

"Thanks," I said.

"It's your funeral," Kecia said.

My GIP guided me to the service exit as I did some emergency hacking, creating a false persona showing me as a citizen. It was a shell job that would get by most security. I was taking the chance that the security in the city was just as laxed as that on the service. If it wasn't, I'd be in trouble in trouble.

I strolled through the docks unnoticed. Every being I passed was full AI, programmed for total subservience to humans. I could take a dump in the middle of the floor and the damn things would be wiping my ass before I finished. The floating city was one huge UC violation, and no one was doing a damn thing about it. I could see the future, first the floaters, then rest. Not on my watch.

I stepped into the fresh air. I was not ready. As much as I didn't want to say it, this fleeking city was beautiful. Never in my life had I seen such well-maintained landscape. It was perfect blend of organic and artificial, so much so it was damn near impossible to tell where the real ended and the fake began. And the people! There were some bodyjocks out there making billions of cryptos off these people. It took me a few minutes to realize I stood out like a hacked drone with my imperfect ass. I shuffled away for cover. I almost made it.

"Hey, you!" someone shouted.

I turned to see a man marching toward me, his chalky face perfectly angry. He grabbed my arm, and I resisted the urge to bust his eye socket.

"Are you cleaning or repair?" he asked.

"Uh . . ." I answered.

"Are you damaged?"

He touched his wrist.

"Repair," I replied.

He swiped his wrist and the coordinates to his condo synced with the GIP.

"We'll be back in an hour. You should be done by then. If not, I'm calling the scrapper."

The man marched away. I kept a blank expression on my face until he were far enough away. This was easier than I thought. Meat bag assumed I was the help because of my flawed appearance.

I found the condo and went inside. I could do what I needed to do without access to his home network, but hacking it would mean less security to avoid, if any. These bags thought they were in paradise. They were about to get a rude awakening.

My initial scan didn't turn up Carlos's name. I switched to visual a second later I got him. I saw his name and laughed out loud.

"Percy Waynewright? What kind of fleeking name is that?"

I gipped his location then began to leave. Then I remembered the window. I ambled to the room location, picked up the heaviest thing I could find and busted the other window. Fleeking meat bag.

I'd altered the security video by the time I reached the front door. Carlos's pad was on the other side of the city, which meant I'd have to catch a ride. But I needed to spruce up a bit. It kind of hurt my feeling that that asshole thought I was an AI. I know, the last thing I needed to think about was my appearance, but what can I say? I pinged a ride and seconds later it arrived as if it was just waiting for me to call. I hopped in and swiped the directions to the nearest boutique.

The salesclerk gave me the same look the asshole did when I entered the shop. He forced a perfect smile on his face as he approached. I could tell he'd scanned my data because his smile was almost genuine by the time he reached me.

"Welcome to Vickie's Couture, Miss May," he said.

I waved him off as I browsed the holo wardrobe. I stopped before a pantsuit that looked comfortable, a bit stylish and loose enough to hide my weapons.

"This one," I said.

The image faded. I hurried to the dressing room. As I suspected, this was a tailor.

"Please disrobe," the tailor drone asked.

I took off my clothes and the tailor took measurements.

"Your outfit will be ready momentarily," the tailor said.

The walls transformed into an ocean scene, complete with crashing waves, seagull sounds and jumping whales. I was fascinated for a moment; I've never been to the ocean, and the graphics were so lifelike I could feel the humidity. I sat in the chair and closed my eyes. Listening to the roaring waves relaxed me, and gods know I needed it.

"Miss May, your outfit is ready."

I opened my eyes disappointed. Not with the outfit; it looked great and fit perfectly. I was disappointed because I was back on the clock. I hacked the boutique's net and downloaded the beach code. Never know when you might need a little more rest.

The salesclerk was waiting as I exited the dressing cube.

"You're gorgeous!" she exclaimed.

"Yeah, right," I replied. I swiped the funds to the boutique then hailed a lift to Carlos's flat. The lift streaked me over the city, perfectly synced with the light traffic. So, this was the high life. I had to admit I could see the appeal. But I also knew the consequences. Everything going on here could be available to everyone in the UC if certain people didn't see obscene profits in it.

The lift gained altitude as we approached an organic skyscraper. At least these shits still believed in sustainability. The lift took me to a landing pad on top of the building. Carlos's flat pinged and I exited, and the lift took off. He was doing way better than I imagined.

I cracked the security codes to the building just in case Carlos wasn't home and I had to wait for him. I entered the building; it seemed Carlos had an entire floor to himself.

My sensors told me he was inside. I pressed the doorbell and waited.

"Just leave it," he said. Five cryptos appeared in my account.

"Cheap ass," I whispered.

The door slid open. Carlos stood before me in a pair of silk drawers and nothing else.

"Look, I don't have time for . . ."

His mouth dropped open and his eyes went wide.

"Long time no see, Percy," I said. I pushed my way into his flat.

Carlos followed me to his kitchen. I opened his fridge and began searching for something to eat.

"Michelle, what are you doing here? How did you find me?"

I realized why Carlos ordered out. The fridge was empty except for a six pack of beer and a box of old fried rice. I ambled over to his couch then plopped down on it.

"The real question is, what the fleek are you doing here?" I asked. "Living with the same people trying to burn your ass? Not smart, doll."

"It's worked so far, two years to be exact," Carlos replied. "It's the last place they'd look."

"Good thing they're not as smart as me," I said. "Once I figured out you were living the highlife it didn't take long to track you down, Percy."

"Well, it's your job to find people," Carlos said. "Now that you've ruined my day, why are you here?"

Carlos's question sobered me up.

"I'm in trouble and I need your help," I said.

"Does it have anything to do with this?" He waved his hand around.

"Yes, sort of," I replied.

"I'm out," Carlos said. "Get out of my flat."

"No," I said. "You owe me."

"I don't owe you shit," Carlos said. "I appreciate you letting me walk with the cryptos, but it's not like you did everything yourself. Fleek, you could have kept half, but you wanted to be all high and mighty."

My face was on fire, I was so angry.

"It's not about the fleeking money!" I shouted. "It's about our world. It's about everything the Hackers fought for going down the shitter. That's what it's about!"

"Get out, Michelle," Carlos said. "Find somebody else to help you."

Those last words hit me like a sledgehammer to the chest. I felt my eyes watering and I tried to hold back.

"That's just it," I said, my voice weak. "You're it. You're my last chance."

The tears came and it made me angrier. I stomped toward his door.

"Michelle wait," he said. He grabbed my arm, and I yanked it free.

"Don't fleeking touch me!" I said.

The door slid open, and two security drones flew it. They scanned me before I could blink.

"Michelle Carter, you have been identified and charged with forced entry and burglary. Please accompany us to the nearest security precinct for processing."

Even their security drones were polite. A wave of resignation swept over me. I was tired of running, tired of fighting, tired of this life. Maybe I was stupid trying to resist what was coming. At that moment I didn't care. I just wanted it over.

I shrugged and followed the drones into the hallway. We were almost to the stairs leading to the roof when the drone to my right exploded. I dropped to my knees and snatched out my bolter as the second drone shattered. I spun around to see Carlos with a bolter in his hand and a smirk on his face.

"Come back inside," he said.

I lowered my bolter.

"Thank you, Carlos," I said.

"Don't thank me yet," he replied.

I walked back inside, following Carlos into his room. He went into his walk-in closet and emerged with three bags.

"Planning on going somewhere?" I asked.

Carlos laughed.

"I knew this was going to end one day," he replied. "So, I had a contingency plan."

We were leaving his room when the door buzzed. Our hands went to our bolters.

"Yeah," Carlos said.

"Pizza," a voice responded.

Carlos pulled up his screen then tapped the pay button.

"Thank you for choosing Jake's Pizza," the voice responded.

The door slid open. The pizza sat on the floor, the aroma setting off my stomach. Carlos picked up the pizza, took it to his bar then sat it down.

"What are you doing?" I spoke. "We need to bolt."

"Sit down," he said. "I got this. Besides, I'm starving and I'm sure you are, too. Best eat now since we don't know the next time, we'll get a chance."

He had a point. I took a seat and opened the box while Carlos fished a couple of beers from his fridge. I looked at the pizza scowled. It was piled high with whatever type of meat still existed and a few new processed ones. I'd been vegan for ten years.

"I don't eat flesh," I said. Carlos grinned as he opened his beer.

"This might be your last day alive," he said.

I shrugged and grabbed a slice. I bit it and moaned. I forgot how good meat tasted. We finished off the pizza and drank two more beers. I was stuffed, buzzing and in no shape to fight anybody. This was a bad decision.

"We have to go," I said.

"Just wait a few more minutes," Carlos said.

"Wait for what?"

I was answered by Carlos's buzzing wrist.

"I'm here," a woman said.

"Coming out now," Carlos answered. "I have a friend."

"What?"

The door swished open. Standing before it was Kecia.

"You!" she said.

"Y'all know each other?" Carlos asked.

"We met a few minutes ago," I said.

"Met hell!" Kecia said. "She highjacked me."

Kecia wagged her finger at me.

"All you had to do was tell me you knew Percy."

"I wasn't sure if Car . . . I mean Percy was here."

Kecia carried two sets of coveralls under her arm, she handed them to Carlos.

"Put these on," she said then looked at me. "Yours might fit big."

I slipped the coveralls over my clothes. They were loose, but I could manage. Kecia gave us a quick inspection then led us to her lift on the roof.

"This is gonna cost you extra," Kecia said.

"I'm good for it," Carlos replied.

"Are you good for it right now?" Kecia said.

"Fleek!" Carlos rolled up his sleeve, exposing his screen. He swiped the cryptos to Kecia.

"Thank you," she said.

"Greedy ass," Carlos replied.

She laughed then we lifted off. As she steered the lift into the air lanes, five black personal lifts streaked by then landed on the roof.

"Who the fleek are they?" Kecia said.

A chill swept through me.

"They're looking for me," I said. "You might want to get us out of here fast."

"Not too fast," Carlos corrected. "We'll look suspicious."

"Gotcha," Kecia said.

Kecia sped up a little then worked her way to ground level. A few minutes later we descended into the supply hangar.

"There's a food shuttle due in five minutes," she said. "Walk around and act like you know what you're doing until then. The coveralls have your pass data embedded so no one will ask any stupid questions."

Kecia glared at me. "I hope I never see you again."

"You can count on it," I replied.

Kecia took off and we hurried to the commissary truck station.

"So, what's your plan?" Carlos asked.

"I'll tell you once we get on . . ."

A powerful explosion shook the hanger. I looked toward the direction of the sound and saw Kecia's transport spiraling to the ground like a burning metal bird. The five personals that passed us earlier followed it down.

"Come on!" I yelled.

I grabbed Carlos's arm, dragging him through the hanger to an unguarded cargo lift. We ran inside to the cockpit. A thick man with a ragged beard slept on the control seat. Carlos tapped him on the shoulder, and he woke.

"Hey . . .the fleek you're doing in here?"

Carlos gave him a hard one across the jaw, knocking him out. He picked the man up and tossed him from the lift as I hacked the control panel. I switched to manual and guided the lift from the hangar as Carlos took a seat beside me. We descended into Newlanta, and I steered the ship to a quiet street in the Dump then set it down. The door lifted and Carlos headed for the nearest cover, a beat-up lift about a block away. I sprinted to the nearest alleyway on the opposite side of the street, grinning as I took out my bolter. Carlos was a vet of being on the run and we both knew the best way to slow down hunters was to make sure they couldn't hunt. The black lifts appeared moments later; two hovering overhead while the other three landed. The agents climbed out their vehicles and it took me everything in my power not to scream in rage. They were wearing UCS uniforms, soiling them with their corrupt asses.

"Stay focused," Carlos's voice chirped in my ear. "I'll take the ones up top. You deal with others."

I answered with a nod. Carlos put his bolter back into his jacket then lifted his right arm. His hand folded back, revealing his heavy gun. I was impressed; I didn't detect it at all. Carlos dropped a lot of cryptos for that kind of tech, which meant he never intended on living the glamorous life forever. Like they say, you take the doll out of the Dump . . . well, you know the rest.

Carlos waited until all the agents were in the stolen lift before blasting the others out of the sky. And when I say blast, I mean it. The first lift exploded into a shower of metal and meat. The second lift attempted to escape but Carlos popped it, sending the craft into a downward spiral. It crashed a few meters from the cargo lift. I was so stunned I almost missed the agents running out of the lift, firing wildly. I took two down before Carlos blew the rest away. We both held our positions for a few clicks just in case anyone survived even though we both knew otherwise. I stepped from cover then waved at Carlos; his bolter folded back into place.

We fled the carnage. Salvagers would be on the scene before the constables and break everything down in less than five minutes as soon as we turned the corner. That would give whoever was tracking me a merry chase and give me and Carlos time to disappear, at least temporarily.

"So, where we going?" Carlos asked.

"I'm trying to figure that out," I said.

"I know a place," Carlos said. "We can lay low as long as we need. That should be enough time for you to tell me the plan."

"Lead the way, Percy," I said.

Carlos scowled. "You don't have to keep calling me that, you know."

"I know," I replied. "It's fun, though."

Carlos took point, walking with purpose.

"So where are we going?" I asked.

"There's a free bunk nearby," he said.

I stopped, a wave of fear washing through me."

"Fleek no," I said.

Carlos turned to glare at me.

"You got a better idea?" he asked.

"Not right now," I said. "Give me a minute."

"You ain't got a minute," Carlos said. "You need a lot of rest and time to think things through."

"Don't tell me what I need," I shot back. "I've been on the run for three years. You been with me three hours and suddenly you know what I need?"

"How long you been biting clouds?" he asked.

I froze. "What are you talking about?"

"Don't shit with me," Carlos said. "I noticed it the minute I saw you. How long?"

All my energy drained through my feet and into the ground.

"I don't know," I confessed. "Ten days?"

"More like a month, I'm guessing," Carlos replied. "We're going to a free bunk. Period."

Carlos reached for my arm, and I pulled away. A free bunk would cut us off completed from the net. All my systems would shut down; we'd have no contact with the outside world. The thought of hearing only my own thoughts was terrifying.

"I can't," I said.

"Then do this shit without me," Carlos said. "I'm not risking my life with your geeked up ass."

"I can handle it!" I said a little too excited.

"Clean Michelle is the baddest bitch I know," Carlos said. "I don't know about the person I'm looking at now. I ain't risking my life on it."

"So why are you with me now?" I asked.

"Returning the favor," Carlos said. "Which means getting that shit out of your system. If you refuse, I'm out. No sense in both of us dying."

I knew I was fleeked. But I was scared. To be cut off from everything was something I'd never experienced, something I didn't want to experience. I'd heard it drove people mad, and it was a form of torture among the Underground. I had no choice though. As much as I hated to admit it, I needed Carlos to help me. It was the only way I stood a chance at stopping what was coming.

"Okay," I said. "Let's do it."

I followed Carlos into a maze of alleys and barren streets until we ended up at a dilapidated building in the center of the Dump. I was surprised it still stood; UC Upgrade was very thorough about renovating structures.

"How does this still exist?" I asked Carlos.

"Because you can't see it," Carlos replied.

"It's a big fleeking building," I said. "It's right here."

"But you can't 'see' it," Carlos said again, and then I got it.

"This building's been around before the Collapse," I said.

"Bingo," Carlos replied. "No smart materials inside or out. Straight analog, if that much. The folks that live in it keep it that way."

"How did you find out about this?" I asked him.

"After I split up with you, I decided I needed to lay low to make sure I wasn't on anybody's shit list. I dropped a few cryptos here and there and this turned up."

"Is this the only one?"

"Nah. There are thousands of them scattered across the UC. A lot of people out there want to be invisible, and this is where they go to do it."

I made a mental note. If I ever got back to my old self, I'd either make use of this or tear it down.

Carlos led me inside. We crunched over broken glass until we reached a stairwell. I followed him to the ground level then down a dim hallway. Carlos stopped before a door.

"We're home," he said. He reached into his pocket then pulled out a metal object.

"What is that?" I asked.

"A key," Carlos replied.

"A what?"

Carlos stuck the metal object into a hole in the door then turned. There was a clicking sound; Carlos grinned then pushed the door open.

"Come on," he said. "Let's get your head straight."

I stepped into the room and my links wavered.

"Carlos, I changed my mind," I said. "Isn't there . . ."

Carlos pushed me inside then shut the door. Everything went blank. All I could see was him. There were no peripheral screens, no holos, no data streams; nothing.

"Welcome home," Carlos said.

I fainted.

When I woke the bunk was filled with an amazing aroma that made me hungry and nauseous. Carlos stood over the micro-stove stirring a pot. He looked at me and grinned.

"Welcome back to the world," he said.

I rubbed my eyes to get them to focus but they wouldn't.

"What's wrong with me?" I said. "Why can't I see straight?"

"That's the last bit of that shit in your system," Carlos replied. "It should clear up in a couple of days. This will help."

He spooned the stew into a bowl, stuck a spoon in it then handed it to me. I took the bowl, and it warmed my shaking hands. One spoonful in my mouth and my hunger and queasiness subsided.

"This shit is good," I said. "I didn't know you could cook."

"I can do a lot of things you don't know about," Carlos replied. "We're not ice like that."

I ate another spoonful. "How long have I been out?"

"A week and a half."

I almost dropped my bowl. "What?"

"A week and a half," Carlos repeated. "Actually, I expected it to take longer. You had a lot of shit in your system. You're strong, though."

I finished the rest of my bowl in silence. For a minute I forgot where I was and tried to call up my stats. The free bunk did its job; I didn't get fleek. It was just me and Carlos, enjoying each other's company. I couldn't wait to get out of that place, danger or not.

Carlos fixed another bowl of stew then sat beside me.

"I love it here," he said.

"You're crazy then," I said.

"Don't you ever just want to get way from all that shit outside?" he said. "You know, live like the ancestors did."

"If it was so great for the ancestors, we wouldn't have done all this," I replied. "Besides, you can't go back. Might as well make the best of the here and now."

Carlos chuckled. "Yeah. We're doing a great job of that."

As I finished my bowl, an idea sprang free in my mind.

"Live like the ancestors," I whispered.

"What?" Carlos asked.

I grinned. "Live like the ancestors. That's what we need to do!"

I put down my bowl and stood on my wobbly legs. "We need to live like our ancestors. We need another revolution."

"Okay, you're still strung out," Carlos said. "I thought I heard you say start a revolution."

"I did," I said. "The elites have a head start but I know how we can catch up."

"I thought the plan would be to lay low until they forgot about you," Carlos said.

"That was your plan, not mine."

Carlos put down his bowl. "Okay, I'll bite. How do you plan to jump off this revolution?"

"Well, we'll need an army first," I said.

"Yeah, right," Carlos replied. "That's the easy part. We'll broadcast on the dark net, hey, we're building an army to start a revolution against the elites trying to restore the old ways. If you like losing your lives for a cause, light us up."

"That shit ain't funny," I said.

"I thought it was," Carlos replied.

"We'll fight fire with fire, asshole. The elites are manufacturing soldiers. We'll beat them to the punch."

"How are we going to do that?" Carlos asked.

"We know the perfect person."

Carlos' eyes drifted up as he thought, then they went wide.

"You can't be serious," he said.

I grinned. "I am."

"She's in prison," Carlos said. "We put her there. Why would she help us?"

"Because we're going to get her out," I replied.

EPISODE FOUR: BREAKOUT

It was good to be alive again. One month in the free bunk was torture to me. I had nobody but Carlos to talk to, no streams to ride, no holos to analyze and worst of all, no trash vids to waste my time. It was all back in shining glory. But on the other hand, what Carlos said was right, but I'll never tell him that. My mind was clearer than it's ever been. The drugs were tearing me down so slowly that I didn't notice the decline. I found him for the wrong reasons, but it saved my life just the same. At least for the moment. Now I planned to jump right back into the shit.

"Who is the person we're looking for again?" Carlos asked.

"Afaafa Selemani," I said. "She's the UCS department liaison. She has access to every division, including security and detention. If anyone knows where Ms. Liu is, she does."

"I thought you said your department is heavily compromised," Carlos said.

"It is," I replied. "If we meet with Afaafa she might turn us in, which is why we're not going to meet with her."

Carlos raised an eyebrow. "You're hacking her systems right now, aren't you?"

I grinned. "Yes, I am. And this shit is complex as fleek."

"So, you can just walk around breaking into folks shit like that," he said. "Damn, woman. No wonder they're trying to kill you."

"It's not that easy," I replied. "They've changed the core security DNA. I've got to figure out the root frame before I can break the system."

"Root frame?"

"Code freaks are lazy," I said. "Once they discover a core helix for coding, they build everything they make on that. Crack the helix and its lottery time. I used to know all the UCS helixes, but they've been replaced."

"Probably because of you," Carlos said. "Damn, thief."

That's one thing I like about Carlos. He makes me laugh. He's the only person that can insult me without ending up with a knot rising on their head.

"Is it hard?" he asked.

"Nah, just different," I answered. "I'm almost there."

Just as I was about to open Pandora's box, I found a surprise.

"Fleek!"

I broke all connections as fast as I could, but I wasn't fast enough. Every muscle in my body clamped shut and I fell. If Carlos hadn't been there, I would have crashed on the street face first.

"Michelle! Michelle!"

His voice sounded like he was talking through a pillow. This was the most powerful RSV I'd ever stepped on. Oh, that's Reactive Security Virus for you meat bags. There was nothing I could do except wait for my repair protocols to kick in. Carlos didn't need instructions. He whisked me to the nearest coffee shop and rented a private pod. He propped me up in a chair then ordered a chai, smirking while I regained control of my body. When I finally felt my face again, I scowled.

"You thought that was funny?" I spoke.

"I knew you'd be alright," he replied. "So, what's the four?"

A wall tile slid opened, and Carlos's chai floated in on the conveyor. I picked it up and drank.

"Hey!" he said.

I finished the chai. "Can't hack in. We're gonna have to do this physically. We're breaking into UCS headquarters."

"Didn't you spend three years avoiding that?" Carlos said. Another chai rolled into the room. I reached for it, and he glared at me. I let it pass.

"No way I could get near that building," I said. "That's why you're doing it."

Carlos rolled his eyes as he sipped his tea.

"I figured." He finished his drink then stood. I tried to stand, but my legs were still wobbly.

"I need to recoup," I said. I swept the net, found a rental vacancy nearby and booked it. The direction dropped into my mem.

"Got us a place. Let's go."

Carlos stepped out of the pod then froze. He held up his hand as he eased back in. The look on his face was not pleasant.

"We have friends," he said.

I hacked the shop's system then linked to their cameras for eyes. Three UCS agents sat in the shop; another five were positioned outside. There was no way we could shoot our way out of this one. Too many agents, too many innocents.

"How did they find us so fast?" Carlos asked

"The virus," I replied.

"What are we going to do?" he asked.

"Give me a sec," I replied.

I attempted to hack one of the agents but failed. It was completely hardwired, probably following an installed code. I jumped into the city grid, looking for a distraction that would give us some time. I found it seconds later.

"Sorry about this," I whispered.

We heard an explosion. Carlos's mouth fell open.

"What the fleek did you just do?"

"I overloaded the local power grid."

The coffee shop went dark. The emergency lights flicked on moments later.

"Take a peek," I said.

Carlos looked outside. "They're gone. Why would they light out after a power grid explosion?"

"I planted a description that resembled me," I said.

"You're crazy," Carlos said.

I grinned. "I know. Now let's go."

We fast-walked out of the coffee shop, buzzed a lift and zipped to our new hideout. Carlos kept watch while I worked on the codes he needed to get into UCS headquarters. A lot had changed, but too much was still the same. After two hours of hacking and splicing I was done.

"Okay," I said. "I built you a history going back ten years. Security won't ping you. Unfortunately, I can't do anything about physical id. You're a big dude."

"I'll worry about that," Carlos said. "Who and what am I looking for?"

"You still have an input?"

"You need to jack me?" he asked.

"Yes," I replied. "I can't trust this to the Storm."

"That's kinda personal," he said.

"Get over here," I fussed. "You're wasting time."

Carlos trudged over to the bed. He took off his shirt, revealing his input at the back of his neck.

"Don't you think that's kind of obvious?" I said.

"This is the first time I've used that thing in years," he replied. "Let's just get it over with."

I took a cord out of my kit then stuck one end into my port under my arm. I hooked up to Carlos then downloaded the file."

MILTON J. DAVIS

"Ouch," he said.

"Baby," I replied.

I unhooked us and tried hard to erase the other info that leaked into my feed.

"You're nasty," I said.

Carlos scowled "See, that's why I didn't want to do that."

"I won't tell anyone," I replied. "It would get me arrested. How's the data?"

Carlos blinked his eyes as he sifted through the file.

"Ice. When do we start?"

"Yesterday," I said.

* * *

Throughout the entire timeline of human existence, one thing remains constant: night shift sucks. Carlos and I sat in a lift a few blocks from UCS headquarters, waiting for the shift change. I watched the entrance on my holomonitor as Carlos tugged and pulled at his UCS uniform, a frown on his face.

"Remind me never to use Tony Tailors again," he said.

"It was the best choice at such a short notice," I replied. "Not bad for a three-minute stitch."

"You wear this shit then," Carlos said.

"Can't. I'm a fugitive, remember?"

The UCS entrance door slid open, and the second shift spilled out into the dark streets.

"Showtime," I said.

Carlos got out of the lift then ambled to the building.

"Make sure you're one of the last to enter, okay?"

"Like I never broke into a place before," Carlos replied.

"You never broke into UCS before," I said.

I hacked into Carlos's vids.

"Ow!" he said. "What the fleek?"

"I need your eyes. Gonna have to give you verbal directions."

"I'm seeing double."

"It's temporary. Now go."

Carlos climbed out of the lift and stumbled down the street. After a few more steps his vision adjusted, and he walked with the confidence of a person who was supposed to be where they were going. Carlos waved at the security officer. The woman waved him in without looking up, her eyes fixed on his data. I'd have to fix that when I returned, if I returned.

"Where to?" Carlos asked.

"Keep down this hall then make a right at the next hallway."

Carlos followed my directions until he stood outside Afaafa's office. He entered and went straight to her computer, took out the translink and inserted my hack flash.

"Excuse me, what are you doing in my office?"

Carlos spun around to see Afaafa standing in her doorway, her hands on her narrow hips.

"Fleek" I said.

Carlos took the flash out of her console and put it in his pocket. He smiled then ambled to Afaafa, his hand extended.

"Hello Ms. Selemani. I'm from IT. I was told you were having problems with your console."

I must admit, Carlos was smooth, but Afaafa wasn't convinced.

"I didn't call IT," she said. "If I didn't have to work nights this week, I wouldn't have caught you here."

"I got a work order. I'm just doing my job," Carlos said. "And I'm done."

Carlos walked to the door, but Afaafa stopped him, putting her hand on his chest.

"Swipe me your work order," she said.

"I don't think Michelle would want me to do that," he replied.

"Carlos!" I shouted in his head. "What the fleek are you doing?"

I watched Afaafa eyes go wide before she spoke.

"Michelle? Oh, my Spirits, Michelle?"

Afaafa went behind Carlos then shoved him out of her office.

"Get away from me! I'm giving you thirty minutes to get out of this building before I report a break in."

Carlos fast walked down the hall.

"Wait!" Afaafa called out.

"Don't wait," I said. "Get out of there."

Carlos stopped and turned to Afaafa.

"What?"

"Michelle," she said. "I hope you're safe. A lot of us do."

I was crying before I realized it. I was still crying when Carlos entered the lift.

"Looks like you still have a few friends on the inside," Carlos said.

"She shouldn't have done that," I replied, wiping the tears from my cheeks. "She might have put herself in danger."

"Her choice," Carlos said. "Let's make sure we don't fleek this up, so her gesture won't be in vain."

Carlos handed me the flash as our lift sped off. I linked to it then jumped into the data. I didn't like what I found.

"She's on Luna," I said.

Carlos laughed. "I'm sorry. I thought I heard you said Ms. Liu is on Luna."

"That's what I said."

"What the fleek is she doing on Luna?"

"UCS high security petitionary," I replied. "Which makes no sense. That facility is reserved for the criminally insane and high-level hackers. Liu's crime was low level tech."

"I guess we're screwed," Carlos said.

"Not necessarily," I replied. I closed my eyes, cursing silently to myself. "I can get us there."

"You're shitting me," Carlos said. "You can get us off planet?"

"Yes," I replied.

"Cow shit," Carlos shot back. "There's not that much hacking in the net. You'd have to know somebody."

"I do," I said. "My ex-husband."

*   *   *

It was the hardest link I ever made. Timothy hated me for all the right reasons. We made promises to each other, and I didn't keep mine. Part of it was the job, but most of it was me. And now I was about to contact him to ask for a favor that involved the main reason why he left me. I wasn't even sure he would take my link, but I was hoping he would only because he and the kids haven't heard from me for years. He would probably answer only to curse me out. But it was my last shot. Maybe after things settle down, we could talk about getting back together, I thought. Or maybe not.

"Fuck do you want?" were the first words out of his mouth. Despite the anger, it was good to hear his voice.

"Hi Tim. How are the kids?"

"They're kids. They're coping."

"How are you?"

"Like you care."

"I do."

"We haven't heard from you for three years."

"Shit is bad, Tim." I hesitated for a minute, fighting to keep my voice from breaking. "Things are bad at the unit. I've been accused of things I didn't do. I've been running and hiding for years."

There was a long silence before Tim spoke.

"That's cow shit," he finally said.

"I promise it's true," I replied. I heard the desperation in my voice and was ashamed.

"I've seen the net," he said. "They're talking about corruption within your department. They didn't give names, but I didn't care. I knew you weren't one of them. You care more about that fleeking unit than you do about your own family."

"No, I don't," I said. "There's no way I could. I miss you all every day."

"The kids hate you, you know," Tim said. "I've tried my best to explain to them what happened, but they won't listen. All they know is that you left them; you left us."

I muted myself before I began crying.

"This is taking too long," Carlos said. "Ask him already."

"Fuck you!" I replied. I wiped my eyes.

"Tim, I need a favor."

He didn't respond. He was still on the link, so I kept talking.

"I need to get on Luna," I said. "There someone there that can get me out of this."

"Goodbye, Michelle," Tim said. "Good luck."

"Tim, wait!"

He broke the link.

"What's the deal?" Carlos asked.

"He broke the link," I said. "He won't . . . wait a minute."

There was an attachment to our call. I downloaded it then transferred it to my secure drive before opening it.

Michelle. We've been under surveillance ever since you disappeared. I don't understand why you left us, and I probably never will. I still love you and so do the children. I hope you can clear your name and come back to us. I can't help you, but there is someone who can. Be careful.

I opened the data link.

"You ever heard of a Drago Stanovich?"

"That's our contact?" Carlos asked.

"Yes."

Carlos sat down on his bed and began rubbing his forehead.

"What?" I asked.

"This is dirty," he said. "Deep dirty."

"It's our only way onto Luna," I said.

Carlos continued to stare at the floor. He took a deep breathe before looking up at me.

"Okay," he said. "But I'll handle this. Give me all the details and no piggybacking. Understand?"

I'd never seen Carlos so serious, and it scared me.

"Uh, maybe we should look for another way."

"If Drago is involved, it's the only way," Carlos said. "When it goes down, I don't want you anywhere near it."

"But we're a team."

"Not on this one," Carlos replied. "Once you deal with Drago, you'll get a stink on you that never goes away. You have a life and a family. You don't need that burden."

"Maybe I can . . ."

"No," Carlos said. "I do this, or it doesn't get done. I'm going to need a few things though."

"Name it," I said.

"I need you to upgrade my reactive boards and tweak my weapons systems. I'm also going to need the highest-level antivirus you can get."

"All we need is a way to Luna," I said. "You're prepping to go to war."

"I am. That's the only way you deal with Drago. It's the only thing he understands. It might get messy. If it does, you know what to do."

We got to work. Carlos took me to a hack shop in the Dump, a place where cryptos buy silence. I had to knock him out to make some of the hardware upgrades, which meant he needed healing time. We returned to the room where we spent the next day preparing. I kept asking Carlos if I could piggyback and he kept saying no. It was a front, of course. I installed shadow codes while doing the upgrades. I was just hoping he'd finally say yes so I wouldn't feel so bad once he discovered them.

We took a jacked lift to Drago's spot, a huge analog warehouse near the edge of the Newlanta dome. I let Carlos out three blocks from the building and he walked the rest of the way. I was watched him from one of my microdrones when he spoke.

"I changed my mind," he said.

"About what?"

"I'm going to need your eyes once I get inside. Can you do that?"

"Maybe. Depends on their security."

"Ice," he said. "Whatever you see, don't hold it against me."

I got worried.

"Carlos, what are you planning?"

"Don't worry about it," he said. "Just be ready."

Drago's dolls began trailing Carlos about a block away from the building. By the time he reached the entrance twelve of them surrounded him. This was a bad idea. Carlos was going to be dead before he stepped in the door.

"You got me?" he said.

My hands shook. "Carlos, I don't think . . ."

"Just keep an eye on me, okay?"

"Okay."

I landed my drone in the hair of one of the dolls as they escorted Carlos into the warehouse. The moment he stepped inside my heart sank. The hallway was lined with heavily armed dolls and cyborgs, each one staring at Carlos. This was a set up. Carlos was dead, I would be soon. But I couldn't leave him. He'd want me to run, but I wasn't going anywhere. He knew what was going down, which is why he had me juice him up. He probably thought he could get the intel then fight his way out. There was no way, at least not alone.

I strapped on my gear and check my weapons. I did a quick dive into the Shadows, loading up on defensive viruses. It had been a good run. Three years was a long time to dodge UCS. I was tired of running, and I wasn't going to let Carlos go out like that. I guided the lift to within a block of the warehouse then waited as I switched back to my drone. Carlos stood before a hulking doll that sat on a throne behind a wide mahogany desk.

"Carlos Mejia, it's been a long time."

"It has."

"You must be in some deep doo-doo to come to me."

"Something like that. I need a favor."

"You know the rules. A favor for a favor."

"Ice."

Drago leaned back in his chair as he intertwined his fingers.

"You go first."

"I need to get on Luna to pick up a package," Carlos said.

"How big a package?"

"Trunk size."

Drago smirked. He closed his eyes for a second then swiped his right hand. The codes appeared in Carlos's dbank.

"Done. My turn. I want that UCS agent you've been running the streets with."

My mouth went dry. How did he know?

I watched Carlos grin at Drago as his voice filled my head.

"It's been real. Get the fleek out of here!"

He raised his left arm and his bolter appeared. He fired two rounds into Drago's chest as he leaped over the table then ducked for cover. The dolls began shooting, the table ripped apart by their fire. Carlos's hand went out of frame then returned with an EMP. He threw it over Drago's desk.

"Night, night."

The EMP flashed and my vid feed went blank. I jumped out of the lift then sprinted to the warehouse. I pushed the door open and was greeted with the sound of small explosions. Carlos had slipped one of his antique handguns into the building. The EMP knocked out the dolls and damaged the cyborgs. Carlos's left arm was out of action, but he didn't need it. I knelt, taking the Sig Saur from my ankle holster. Carlos wasn't the only one with back up.

As I crept through the building, the full weight of what Carlos was doing hit me. He was killing everyone in the warehouse. It was then I realized that Carlos, my friend, was one of the bad guys. I knew he wasn't a saint; his former profession required a bit of callousness. But I didn't know he had it in him to clean house like this, and that made me a little scared. No; it made me a lot scared.

I found him where his massacre began, behind Drago's desk. Drago was still alive, his meat bag mind trapped in his doll frame. Carlos was prying open his braincase.

"Carlos." I said.

He jumped up then took aim at me. I raised my hands.

"Fleek, Michelle! I told you to run!"

"I couldn't leave you alone," I said, my voice weaker than I wanted it to be. Carlos lowered his gun.

"Since you're here, help me crack this egg."

I took the tool from Carlos then opened Drako's cranium compartment. Before I could ask him what he was planning he literally blew his brains out. Seconds later the EMP effects diminished, and everything came back online. Carlos used Drako's sleeve to wipe brain matter off his clothes.

"Is the data good?" he asked.

It took me a minute to focus and inspect it. Everything checked out.

"It's good," I said.

"Let's go."

We hurried back to the lift then headed for our destination; Newlanta Skyport. Carlos sat quietly; his head leaned back on the headrest. I let the lift drive.

"We gonna talk about it?" I asked.

"Talk about what?"

"What just happened?"

Carlos shrugged. "Nothing to talk about."

"The fleek it isn't!"

Carlos looked at me, his eyes narrowed.

"You know who I am. You know what I do."

I turned away.

"I've never seen you do it like that."

"You heard the man ask me to kill you, right? Do you think it made a difference whether I did it or not? You got a target on you. Drago is the kind of person who would kidnap your family and kill them one by one until you gave yourself up, then kill the rest of them anyway. When you go to war with him, it's all or nothing. So, I gave him my all, and now he's nothing."

"Just like that?"

Carlos turned away. "Exactly like that."

"I don't really know you," I said.

"No, you don't," Carlos replied. "But what you do know is that I'm with you on this. You saved my life, and that's more than anyone has ever done for me. Don't be worrying about what I might do to you."

"I wasn't thinking that," I lied.

"Yes you were," Carlos said. "So where are we headed?"

Carlos was done talking about his one-man massacre. I was still shaking, but I had to focus. I called up the data then splashed it on the lift windshield.

"Looks like a cargo transport area," I said.

"Drago probably owned it," he replied.

I dipped into the clouds. Print scrolled under the image.

"He does . . . I mean he did. It's a commissary supplier for the Luna pen and a few of the orbiting stations. Probably a cover for illicit drugs and other contraband."

Carlos laughed. "Probably?"

I went to work creating credentials to get us on a shuttle. Carlos placed his hand on my shoulder.

"Save your energy. We won't be needing all that."

He reached into his pocket and took out a small disc. Drago's face was engraved on the surface.

"He had his own currency?" I said.

"Yep. Vain bitch. Anyway, this will get us where we need to go."

"You sure?"

Carlos nodded. I shrugged and shared the direction with the lift. We were halfway to our destination when I realized I was hungry.

"We need to stop," I said.

"For what?" Carlos asked.

"I'm hungry."

Carlos laughed. "I am, too. We'll take care of all that once we reach the base."

"I'm not looking forward to base food," I said.

"This is Drago's spot," he replied. "You know they'll hook us up."

The lift reached the cargo station. We pulled up to the security gate then waited for the roar of a departing shuttle to die down before talking to the guard. Her stern face appeared on our windshield.

"May I help you?"

Carlos leaned close to the camera.

"We're visiting Drago Enterprises," he said.

"Data?" she asked.

Carlos and I swiped our info. The guard frowned.

"I don't see you on the list."

Carlos held up the coin. "Can you look again?"

The guard's eyes went wide, and she disappeared. The gate opened and the lift pinged, indicating that security clearances had been coded. We cruised across the base to a building and lift pad on the opposite side of the base. Three armed guards approached as we eased into the drop off and the lift doors opened.

"This is my playground," Carlos said. "Let me handle this."

"Are you going to kill anybody?" I asked.

Carlos grinned. "We'll see."

The guards' bolters were pointed down, which was encouraging. One of them, a tall ivory colored man with a low mohawk, stepped forward.

"Carlos Mejia and Michelle Carter? I'm Derrick Jones, your escort."

"Good to meet you," Carlos said. "Let's go."

We followed the guards into the building. The halls were filled with humans, cyborgs and A.I. rushing about. Apparently, Drago did a lot of business off world, which was disturbing. My utopia wasn't all it seemed to be.

We entered a small, automated office area. A brown man with fading hair and thick eyebrows sat behind a transparent security wall. He saw us and waved us in.

"Welcome," he said. I'm Antonio Diego. Sit."

Carlos and I took a seat in front of the desk.

"So, you headed to Luna?" he asked.

"Yes," Carlos said. "We need drop equipment and a large trunk."

Antonio grinned. "Planning on making a withdrawal?"

"Something like that," Carlos replied.

Antonio's smile faded. "That's risky. UCS looks the other way when it comes to us as long as we follow their rules."

"I'm sure this isn't the first time you broke those rules," Carlos replied.

Something wasn't right. I could feel it. Antonio stood and paced.

"And Drago is good with this?" he asked.

"He gave his approval," Carlos said.

Antonio stopped pacing then smirked.

"That would be difficult, since he's dead."

Carlos grinned. "Guess who killed him?"

Antonio stepped away from the desk.

"My men are on their way!" he said.

"You're already dead if you don't call them off," Carlos replied.

I was already hacking, blocking the building's systems, and setting up false credentials. I didn't know exactly how Carlos would play this, but I had an idea. When his UCS holo-badge appeared, I knew my hunch was right.

"Now that Drago has been eliminated," Carlos said. "The UCS expects your full cooperation."

"Of . . . of course," Antonio replied.

"We need a shuttle prepared and ready to go yesterday," Carlos said. "We also need an A.I. orbital pad in position near Luna ready to receive us when we arrive."

"Done," Antonio said.

Carlos and I stood.

"Thank you for your cooperation," Carlos said. "It will be noted in our report."

Antonio went to his console and issued orders. Carlos looked at me.

"You got this, right?" he said.

"You know it," I replied. "You kill people; I hack stuff."

"That was uncalled for," he said.

"But it's true," I replied.

Antonio looked up with a relieved smile.

"Everything's set," he said. "Follow me."

We trailed Antonio down an empty hallway that ended at double doors.

"After you," he said.

"Uh uh," Carlos replied. "You first."

Antonio shrugged then opened the door. He glanced back, then ran.

"Down!" Carlos shouted.

I was way ahead of him. My left knee hit the plascrete as I reached behind my back for my hand bolter then took a bead on Antonio. Carlos beat me to it, blasting the man across the chamber with his arm. Eight security goons laid down a barrage as we scrambled for cover, Carlos heading left, me rolling right. I dipped behind a stack of crates, taking a minute to get my Sig from my ankle holster. I waited for a pause in the shooting then peeked over the crates. The guards were recharging when I lit them up with bolts and bullets. I looked to my left and grinned; Carlos stood in the open, his reactive armor deflecting the bolts while he mowed down the other guards. The firefight was over in minutes, but we weren't in the clear. The security alarm shrieked throughout the building, which meant bodies were either clearing the building or heading our way. The shuttle was our only way out. We sprinted to it.

"You got the codes, right?" Carlos asked.

"Yep," I replied. I scanned the shuttle's manifest. "It's loaded and ready to go. Which doesn't make sense if he was ready to ambush us."

"I think he changed his mind on the way," Carlos said.

"I should have picked it up."

Carlos laughed. "Looks like you ain't the only one that's got tricks."

The shuttle door opened. I switched on the control unit and did an inspection as we made our way to the cabin. The overhead roof opened as we strapped in. Four hover drones drifted above ready to gun us down, red warning lights flashing.

"Does this thing armed?" Carlos asked.

I passed the info to him.

"You're not planning on . . ."

"You drive, I shoot," Carlos said.

"But the debris might damage the shuttle!" I shouted.

"Let's hope not," Carlos replied.

He blasted the drones as I launched. Wreckage rattled the shuttle, but no warning lights went off. As soon as we cleared, I punched it, and we streaked toward space.

A warning pulse filled my head; I pulled up the screen to see three attack drones tracking us, but they were too slow and out of range. As we burned through the atmosphere, I turned my attention to our destination. According to the codes, we were clear.

"That went well," Carlos said.

"Fleek," I replied. "I'd like to see your idea of going bad."

"No, you don't" Carlos said.

We laughed then settled in for a long trip to Luna.

* * *

Luna resembled a pitted pearl below us. I sat at the control panel, making sure our visit to the surface would go without a hitch. No craft of any kind was allowed at the penitentiary, so we had to take a jump elevator. I created our credentials while Carlos kept a look out for any pursuers. So far, we were clean. Either we weren't worth the trouble or they were terrified. I think it was a little of both.

A chime went off in my head, letting me know our docs were approved.

"It's show time," I said.

We donned our jump suits then stood by the elevator with a large transport trunk, waiting for the portal to open. The chamber sealed and the portal slid open. I gave Carlos the thumbs up, and he shoved the trunk out.

When he looked at me, I could see the sweat on his forehead.

"You sure this is going to work?" he said.

"Yes," I replied. "The suits contain deceleration tech. They will adjust as we reach maximum acceleration then ease us onto the touchdown pad."

"And if they don't?"

I clapped my hands together.

"Splat."

"Fleek."

I laughed. "Don't worry. The suit will do everything. Just stay relaxed and let it do its thing."

"What if something goes wrong?" Carlos asked. "Is there a manual override?"

"Yes, but you don't want to do that," I said. "Nothing will go wrong. Promise."

Our conversation was interrupted by the elevator A.I.

"Package touchdown complete. Please enter elevator and commence descent."

Carlos gave me a pathetic look.

"Michelle, maybe you should . . ."

I grabbed his arm then jumped into the tube. I let my body go limp and the suit took over, shifting me into a headfirst descent. I looked to my right; Carlos tumbled end over end.

"Carlos!" I shouted. "Go limp!"

A minute later his body shifted, and he was streaking down like me.

"Thanks," he said.

We plummeted to the platform like diving hawks. About halfway down our suits shifted us again, flipping us to feet first. My soles warmed as the deceleration jets ignited; I felt a light pressure when the magnetic braking kicked in from elevator interior. We touched down beside the trunk like feathers.

The overhead door sealed, and the room was flooded with oxygen. Carlos and I took off our helmets. He switched on the trunk; a set of wheels emerged from the bottom and guidance linked to his wristband. I scanned the pen data for Ms. Liu's location.

"Got her. Let's go."

The entry door slid aside, and we froze. A wide hallway stretched out before us; the walls covered with paintings. Modern statues lined the corridors that teemed with elites accompanied by perfect dolls.

"Are we in the right place?" Carlos asked.

I checked my codes.

"Yes, this is it."

"This isn't a prison. It's a fleeking pleasure resort!"

A pair of scantily clad dolls approached us. My hand went to my bolter tucked in my back holster; Carlos powered up his arm. The dolls smiled, oblivious to our prep.

"Welcome to Olympus," they said in unison. "You have a delivery for Ms. Liu, yes?"

"Ah, yes," I replied.

"Excellent," they said. "Please allow us to escort you to her suite."

They walked away and we followed.

"Suite?" Carlos said. "What the fleek is this?"

"A cover," I replied. "Ms. Liu wasn't imprisoned. She was rewarded."

A knot formed in my stomach, and I stumbled.

"You okay?" Carlos asked.

"I'm fine," I replied.

But I wasn't. The more I saw of this place, I worse I felt. A pain hit my head like a bolt, and I teetered toward the wall. My hands felt plascrete and I stopped myself from falling. Carlos came to my side. The dolls gave me a curious look.

"Is everything fine?" they asked.

"Is it?" Carlos asked me.

"No," I said. "Everything is not fine. Everything is shit!"

"If you need to relieve yourself, the facilities are not far away," the dolls said.

"Shut the fleek up!" I shouted.

"Calm down," Carlos said. "You're going to blow this."

"It's already blown," I said. My sickness faded away, replaced by a heat in my stomach that pushed into every part of my body. I stood and straightened my clothes. I glared at the dolls.

"Let's continue," I said.

They led us to a suite with gilded double doors.

"This is the residence of Ms. Liu," they said. "Will there be anything else?"

"No," I said.

The dolls grinned then glided away.

"She can see us," Carlos said.

"No, she can't," I replied. "I scrambled her security."

Carlos knocked on the door.

"Who is it?" she called out. "My security is fleeked."

"Maintenance," I said between my teeth.

"Just a minute!" Liu sang.

My anger flowed into my hands. When the door slid open revealing Ms. Liu's face, the tension snapped. I punched her in the face.

"What the fleek?"

Carlos pushed me into the suite then shut the door. I stood over Liu, my foot raised, preparing to stomp her into dust. Liu looked up holding her nose. Her eyes went wide.

"You!" she said. She scrambled away on her back. "Stay away from me!"

Carlos grabbed me.

"That's not what we came here for," he said.

"She's one of them," I said. "We fought a war to save ourselves from them. From their excess. From their greed. From their control!"

I was out of control. I tried to yank free of Carlos's steel grip, but he didn't budge.

"All this time, all these years I thought I was fighting for a purpose," I ranted. "And you rat asses have returned."

Ms. Liu grinned. "Returned? We never went anywhere."

She stood, walked to her refrigerator then took out the ice tray.

"You didn't win a war," she said. "That was the agreed upon lie. The Elites knew they couldn't defeat the Hackers, and the Hackers knew they couldn't survive without the Elites. So, they compromised. The Hackers would claim they won the war. People would get their 'utopia' and the Elites would be left alone to carry on, but with a hefty price tag. And that's how it went for decades before you two came along."

"I didn't do shit," Carlos said. "It was her."

"Shut it," I said. I glared at Liu. "I did my job."

"Yes," Liu said. "The only agent in the UCS that did."

I started for her again and Carlos held me back.

"Don't blame this shit on me!" I yelled.

Liu wrapped the ice in a towel then placed it against her swelling nose.

"You upset the balance," she said. "When you exposed the Elites, the UCS had to do something about it to save face. But the Elites acted first."

"So, you and the others are just here until the dust clears," Carlos said.

"Exactly," Liu answered. "What I can't understand is why are you here?"

"To kick up more dust," I said. I stomped on Carlos's foot. He howled and I was able to pull free. I ran at Liu then landed a right hook on her jaw before she could move. She crumpled to the floor like the sack of shit that she was.

"Fleek!" Carlos said as he rubbed his foot. "You didn't have to do that!"

"Quit bitching and bring the trunk over here," I said.

Carlos limped over with the trunk. He opened the lid, and I picked up Liu then put her inside. We left the suite, weaving our way through the flirtatious dolls to the elevator. Our lift to the platform was slower. We boarded the shuttle; I strapped Liu in, and we were on our way back to Earth. I grinned as we descended. The Elites thought their little war was over. It was just about to begin.

EPISODE FIVE:
REVOLUTION, TOO

The shuttle landed where it began, which was a risk to its passengers. The truth was that there was no other docking that wouldn't bring suspicion. Two of the occupants freed themselves immediately; the third remained strapped to her seat, her face twisted in anger.

"You won't get away with this," Ms. Liu, former owner and CEO of Jiadan Industries said.

"You better hope we do," Michelle Carter replied. "Because if we're caught, you're the first to go."

Michelle's words sapped Liu's anger, replacing it with fear.

"Damn, you're worse than me," Carlos Mejia said.

"She needs to know what's at stake," Michelle replied to him.

"And what is at stake?" Ms. Liu asked. "You already know that your little image of this world was never real. You thought you knew everything, but just like everyone else you didn't know shit."

Michelle lowered her head as she dug her fingers into the seat cushions.

"I might have been naive, but not anymore," she said. "I'm going to make it real, and you're going to help me."

Ms. Liu laughed nervously. "What can I do?"

"You're going to help me build an army," Michelle said.

"That's impossible!" Ms. Liu said.

"We're about to find out," Michelle replied.

"We got other problems," Carlos said. He pointed to the viewer.

Five UCS agents emerged from the shuttle building, fully armored with bolters raised.

Michelle shrugged. "I expected more."

"Still, though, if they know we're here, everybody else knows too," Carlos said. "The noose is tightening."

Michelle rubbed her neck. "Don't say that. Blast them."

"Wait! You can't do that!" Liu said.

"You have a better plan?" Michelle asked.

Liu sighed. "Let me speak to them. I don't want any blood on my hands."

"I don't think that's a good idea," Carlos said.

Michelle took out her bolter then pressed it against Liu's head.

"Let her," Michelle said. She looked Liu in the eyes. "Like I said, you first."

Liu cleared her throat, her eyes on the bolter pressed to her head. Carlos gave his seat to her, and she activated the comm.

"Officers, this is Ms. Liu Jiaying. I'd like to speak with your commander."

"Ms. Liu are you okay," a voice answered.

"I am. Is this the commanding officer?"

"Yes. I'm Spec Seven Angela Givens. Ms. Liu, we have reason to believe you are in the presence of two known fugitives, Michelle Carter and Carlos Mejia. Can you confirm?"

"Two?" Carlos said. "Fleek!"

Michelle chuckled. "What did you expect?"

"I am in no danger," Jiayang said. "The fugitives that apprehended me on Luna were captured and detained at the transfer station. I am safe."

The commander was quiet for a moment before answering.

"Ms. Liu, I can't confirm your information. The transfer station is not responding." The UCS team raised their bolters.

"I'm confirming it," Jiayang replied.

"You could be under duress," the commander said.

"I assure you that I'm not."

"We request permission to board to confirm," the commander said.

"Talk them out," Michelle said to Carlos. He coded a fire sweep.

"Commander Givens, I'm trying to be reasonable," Jiayang said as she shook her head. "I don't have time for this. Don't force me to go over your head to UCS commander Ghazini. He would not be happy."

Michelle's eyes went wide. "You know Ghazini?"

Jiayang nodded.

"That won't be necessary, ma'am," Givens finally said. The UCS team lowered their weapons.

"Can I at least ask where you intend to go," the commander said.

"Jiadan," Jiayang said.

"That area is restricted, ma'am."

"Not to me."

"It seems you are correct, ma'am. I'm sorry for the inconvenience. You are cleared for departure."

"Carlos," Michelle said. "Get up here and watch Jiayang while I get us out of here."

Carlos squeezed to the back of the shuttle then sat beside Ms. Liu.

"You going to put a bolter to my head, too?"

Carlos grinned. "I don't have to."

Carlos's left hand retracted, revealing his bolter barrel.

The shuttle rose from the landing platform then flew toward Jiadan. Michelle spun around in her seat to gaze at Jiayang.

"How did you know I'd hacked the clearance?"

"Because that's what you do," Jiaying replied. "That's the only way you could have infiltrated Luna. You're the one the UCS is looking for."

Michelle frowned then spun back around.

"I also have supplies on their way to the plant. They should arrive the same time we do."

"What exactly are you planning to do?" Jiaying asked.

"We're building an army," Carlos said.

Jiaying eyes widened. "You can be serious."

Michelle turned around again. "Do you see me smiling?"

"I can't help you," Jiayang said. "The manufacturing codes have probably been changed since I was confined."

Michelle laughed. "That's what you call that? I'll bet the only thing that's been change is the security codes."

"And if you're wrong?"

"Then we kill you and go to plan B," Michelle said.

* * *

Michelle circled the Jiadan facility twice before setting down. The supply trucks were parked at the gate, the driverless vehicles waiting for permission to enter. The trio climbed out of the shuttle, their heel clicks echoing off the walls of the abandoned facility. The pad entrance was locked; Michelle hardwired the security and opened it in a matter of seconds. As they entered, she turned on the power, the lights coming to life in ordered succession while they strolled down the halls to the main control facility.

"You're very talented," Jiaying said. "What a waste."

"You would think that," Michelle replied. "I guess you think I should be working for you."

"Of course," Jiaying replied. "I'd pay you well. In fact, I'll make you general manager of this facility. The position pays enough for you to have your own Luna suite."

"You haven't paid attention to anything going on here, have you?" Michelle replied. "Besides, you don't own anything."

"Oh, I've paid attention," Jiaying said. "There's one thing I've learned over the decades, and that's everyone has a price."

"I'm not everyone," Michelle said. "Cryptos mean nothing to me."

"But your family means everything to you," Jiayang replied.

Michelle shoved Jiayang against the wall then took out her bolter.

"Michelle, no!" Carlos said.

Michelle pressed her forearm into Jiayang's neck, cutting off her breath. She pushed her bolter barrel against the woman's forehead.

"We don't need her now," Michelle said. "We're in. I can handle it from here."

"Yeah, but you're not a murderer," Carlos said. "She's fucking with you."

Michelle didn't move. Jiayang struggled to breathe.

"Never, ever mention my family again," Michelle said. "Do you understand?"

Jiayang managed to nod. Michelle released her then stomped away. Jiayang slumped to the floor. Carlos walked up to her then offered his hand.

"That was stupid," he said.

Jiayang took his hand, and he pulled her to her feet.

"Don't make this hard and you'll walk out of here fine," he said.

"Do you really believe that?" Jiayang said. "I'm already dead. The assholes I work with probably think I'm helping you."

"Then help us," Carlos said. "Michelle's a badass, but she ain't gonna kill nobody unless they deserve it."

"And you?" Jiayang asked.

Carlos shrugged. "This is her show. I do what she tells me to do."

"So, you would kill me if she ordered you to?"

"Yep," Carlos replied. "But I'd feel bad about it."

"The two of you are crazy," Jiayang said.

"Michelle might be, but I'm perfectly sane," Carlos replied. "I'm doing a favor for a friend."

They reached the control room. Michelle switched on the equipment then allowed the supply trucks to enter. She stared at Jiayang; the woman joined her at the hologrid.

"I need optimized A.I., Protocol Five," Michelle said.

"That's illegal," Jiayang said. "Our plant doesn't have the authorization . . ."

Michele pulled up her personal screen, punched in a code then swiped it to the grid.

"You do now," she said.

Jiayang punched in the code. Nothing happened.

"What are we waiting for?" Michelle asked.

"Your supplies have to be processed," Jiayang said. "That's going to take a few minutes."

Michelle began pacing. "We don't have much time. They'll be here soon."

Carlos's eyebrows rose. "They?"

"UCS," Jiayang answered. "You don't think they don't know we're, here, do you?"

Carlos glared at Michelle. "I thought you took care of that."

Michelle stopped pacing and grinned. "I did. I figure it will take a strike team about an hour to get here."

"What the fleek, Michelle!" Carlos said. "Is this a suicide mission? Please tell me it's not."

"It's a diversion," Jiayang said. "She's drawing UCS assets here, but she's planning on striking somewhere else."

"Is she right, Michelle?" Carlos asked.

"Yes," Michele replied.

"Fleek! When were you going to tell me?"

"In about an hour," Michelle replied.

Carlos threw up his hands. "Oh, so just leave me out of the loop. I should leave."

Michele went to Carlos, placing her hand on his shoulder.

"I had to," she said, her voice soothing. "To be honest I didn't think we'd make it this far. It took me three years to set this up, but it still had an ice cube's chance in Hell."

"What are you saying?" Carlos asked.

"Switching on this plant set off all kinds of violations," Michelle said. "Whoever infiltrated the UCS is sending all their assets to destroy it. Jiadan was their biggest threat, and now they have a reason to act."

"Which is why I was on Luna," Jiayang said. "I'm the only person that could activate it."

"But once the plant is destroyed, they have no use for you," Michelle said.

Jiayang's smile faded. "They were going to kill me."

"Eventually," Michelle said. "You and your facility are too obvious."

"This is your fault," Jiayang said.

"It is," Michelle said. "I'm sorry, but I can't take it back. You have to make a decision. Sign on with us one hundred per cent or walk away."

"I don't have a choice," Jiayang said. "With you I might die. On my own I will. I'm in."

"Excellent," Michelle said. "Now quit holding back and make this place a fortress."

Jiayang put in her ear pods as her fingers flew across the holoboard. The factory sprang to life, the assembly line constructing A.I. frames at an amazing pace then transferring them to body vats for synth-muscle and nerve construction. Michelle watched for a minute then walked away, gesturing for Carlos to follow.

"Where we going?"

"To welcome our visitors," Michelle said. "We have to make a stop, first."

Carlos followed Michelle to door marked 'Ordinance.' The door slid aside, revealing storage bins with numerical designations.

"Let's go shopping," Michelle said.

"With pleasure," Carlos replied.

Michelle found the battle armor. She located her size then quickly put on the shielding over her clothes. Carlos dressed as well, although he had to abandon the arm shields because they were too tight for his enhanced appendages. They inspected each other then nodded.

"Where to now?" Carlos asked.

"The landing pad," Michelle said. "They'll be here soon."

They ran to the entryway near the pad, arriving as the UCS transport drone arrived. The agents disembarked; they totaled twenty, fifteen wearing light tactical suits, the other five in heavy armor and carrying armor piercing bolters.

"They came hunting for bear," Carlos said.

"Whatever that means," Michelle replied.

The team barely noticed the shuttle. They spread out, moving quickly yet cautiously toward the entrance. Michelle and Carlos turned on their targeting grids.

"You synced?" Michelle asked.

"Yep," Carlos replied.

"Let's do this . . .."

The pad door exploded, showering Michelle and Carlos with metal and glass as they tumbled down the hallway."

"What the fleek!" Carlos said.

"The gods damn drone!" Michelle replied. "It's armed!"

Carlos and Michelle sprinted back to the entrance and met the UCS force entering the building. Carlos's arm bolter opened and he braced before releasing a bolt. The blast knocked the hapless attackers back to the platform. Carlos dodged right and Michelle left, both shooting free hand, driving back the UCS foes. Carlos sent two bolts into the drone; the second bolt causing the vehicle to burst into flames before exploding. The blast took down the rest of the UCS team; Carlos put a few more rounds into them to make sure they were done.

"We got more incoming!" Michelle shouted. "Jiayang, what's the four?"

"A platoon is heading your way," Jiayang said. "I can have fifty more ready in ten minutes."

"Give me access!" Michelle shouted.

"Done," Jiayang replied.

"Fleek!" Carlos said.

Michelle looked up to see a squadron of attack drones descending on the facility. Carlos raised his heavy bolter.

"Focus on the transports," Michelle said. "The less boots on the ground the better."

Carlos fired, taking out the propulsion units of two transports. The craft fell from the sky, crashing on the pad.

"Way ahead of you," Carlos said.

The sound of rapid footfalls came from behind them. They turned to see the Jiadan A.I. platoon running toward them carrying light bolters.

"The last time we saw them, they were chasing us," Carlos said.

Michelle guided the A.I. onto the platform then spread them out to form intersecting fire lines.

"Come on, let's get back to the control center. We have to get out of here sooner than I planned."

They ran back to the center where Jiayang labored at her holoscreen.

"I have another hundred units ready, with fifty more in the queue," she said without taking her attention from the grid. "Their level two; that's the best I could do this fast."

"What does that mean?" Carlos asked.

"It means they're a little better than chafe," Michelle replied. She turned her attention to Jiayang. "So how do we get out of here? The platform is a no go."

Jiayang looked at them with a smirk. "Follow me."

Jiayang coded the system to continue creating and deploying security bots. They fled the control center, ending up in Jiayang's office. She rushed to her desk, punching a number sequence into her old console. The wall behind her desk slid aside, revealing a heavy armored suit and bolter.

"I see you were prepared for the worst," Michelle said.

"It's a dangerous business," Jiayang replied.

She put on her suit with practiced efficiency then punched another code into a wall unit. The floor beneath her desk shuttered and the desk slid aside, revealing an open hatch. Jiayang ran to the hatch then jumped in. Michelle and Carlos looked at each other, Carlos shrugged.

"Fleek it," he said, and jumped in.

Michelle hesitated until a loud explosion rocked the complex.

"Shit."

Michelle jumped into the chamber. She free fell for a moment until an updraft hit her, slowing her fall until her feet touched gently on the padded floor. Carlos and Jiayang stood by a personal hovering over a magnetic track.

The three climbed into the vehicle. To everyone's relief there was room to spare.

Jiayang activated the craft then pulled up navigation.

"Where to," she asked Michelle.

"Vegas," Michelle replied.

Jiayang turned around, a puzzled expression on her face.

"Where is that?" she asked.

Michelle joined her at the nav screen.

"You really are out of the loop."

Michelle stood beside Jiayang and entered a code. A warning sign flashed large and red; Michelle entered more code and the sign disappeared, replace with the map to Vegas.

"The head of the snake," she said.

"How did you find it?" Carlos asked.

"By looking for what wasn't there," Michelle replied. "Every inch of this planet is mapped and coded. Except Vegas. Whoever was trying to hide it did too good a job. It's like a glaring black hole in a sea of lights, if you know what you're looking for."

Jiayang leaned on the console, folding her arms across her chest.

"And just what will we do when we get there? Just walk in and say, 'All of you are under arrest. Assume the position!"

Carlos guffawed and Michelle glared at him.

"She's funny," he said.

"We have the element of surprise," Michelle said. "That will help."

"Seriously?" Jiayang said. "We have no idea what we'll be up against. I don't think you'll be able to hack your way out of this one."

"First of all, I'm glad you said we," Michelle said. "Because I'm going to need you to contact Ghazini and tell him everything."

"That makes no sense," Jiayang said. "He'll be waiting to snatch us."

"Or he'll come to our rescue," Michelle said. "I don't know Ghazini, but I know his reputation. I don't think he's with this takeover. I think he's being quiet because he doesn't know who to trust."

"Was this part of your plan?" Carlos said.

"No," Michelle confessed. "Actually, I thought we could create enough security A.I. to fight our way out."

"So, this is a desperate move," Jiayang said.

Michelle sat then dropped her face into her hands.

"This is it, y'all," she said. "I got nothing left. I've been running and hiding for three fleeking years and I want this to stop. If it's in Vegas, then that's where it will be."

She looked at Carlos, then Jiayang.

"I'm sorry I dragged y'all into this. If things go to shit in Vegas, turn me in and tell them I forced y'all to do this."

"Well, you actually did," Jiayang said.

"I'm with you, sista," Carlos said.

Michelle smiled. "My boy." She looked at Jiayang. "Make the call."

Jiayang nodded. Carlos sat beside Michelle then draped his arm around her shoulder.

"It's going to be ice," he said. "Don't worry."

"It won't," she said. "Either way, I want it over."

"It's done," Jiayang said. "We have a two-hour ride. We might as well rest."

They each found a space in the personal to rest. Carlos fell asleep immediately; Jiayang joined him not long after. Michelle couldn't sleep. She pulled up video of her family on her holo, smiling, laughing, and crying as she watched them in happier times. The time passed quickly; the green flashing arrival light snatched her from her memories.

Carlos stirred as did Jiayang. The three inspected their armor and weapons as the personal lowered onto the Vegas platform. They exited the vehicle guns raised, scanning the area. Michelle moved close to Jiayang.

"You know how to use that thing?" she asked.

"Better than most, but not as good as you or beefcake over there," Jiayang answered.

"Let us do the heavy lifting then," Michelle said. "If the shit looks bad, haul ass. No need for all three of us biting it."

Jiayang glanced at Michelle. "How do you know I won't switch sides?"

"I don't," Michelle replied. "At this point it doesn't matter. We're probably going to die anyway. Whether it's a bolt in the face or the back of the head, it doesn't matter."

"You're a good person," Jiayang said. "I hope everything works out for you. I mean it."

"Will y'all stop bonding and come on?" Carlos said. "I think I found the way out."

Carlos led them to a broken escalator leading to the surface. They emerged into the desert heat which activated the cooling systems in their suites. The shell of the old Luxor Casino loomed over them, the massive light at the pinnacle of the mock pyramid still working after centuries. The other ancient monuments to chance and greed stood dark and silent like tombs. In the distance colorful lights radiated, beckoning them forward.

"That's our target," Michelle said. "Let's stick close to the buildings for cover."

"Might be security lurking inside," Carlos warned.

"It's either that or walk in the open," Michelle said.

"Not much of a choice," Jiayang said.

Michelle ended the argument by walking away. Carlos and Jiayang followed. They crept from casino to casino, working their way down the strip and closer to the source of the light.

They were exiting the fourth building when Carlos tapped Michelle's shoulder.

"Our luck just ran out," he said as pointed ahead. Two transport drones sped toward them, their searchlights sweeping the ground.

"Inside!" Michelle shouted.

They ran into a derelict casino, looking for the best place to defend themselves. Michelle risked detention by activating her neural scans to see what they were up against.

"Fleek!" she said.

"What?" Carlos asked.

"Let me guess," Jiayang said. "Level Ten security A.I.'s."

"Yep," Michelle said.

"How many?" Carlos asked.

"Too many," Michelle replied.

"Fleek," Carlos said. "No use in waiting then."

Carlos trotted out of the building,

"Wait!" Michelle said.

Carlos took out his Sig as his heavy bolter activated. He sent two bolts into the lead transport drone. It fired back wildly, veering away, and crashing into the other transport. Both vehicles spiraled downward then crashed. Michelle and Jiayang joined him.

"Was that your plan?" Michelle said.

"Lucky shot," Carlos said.

A hail of bolts from the wreckage sent them scurrying for cover. Twelve security bots emerged from the wreckage; their durable bodies burned but mostly undamaged.

Michele, Carlos, and Jiayang returned fire. Carlos's heavy bolter damaged the units, but the lighter bolter fire had little effect. The bots pushed them deeper into the building as another transport drone arrived, releasing more bots. Michelle abandoned her bolter for her Sig, the bullets causing more damage.

Bots poured into the building, sending a shower of bolts at them. They couldn't fire back, only seek cover.

"We have to get out of here!" Carlos said.

"Don't you think I know that!" Michelle shouted back.

"I'll draw their fire," Carlos said. "You two can find a way out the other side."

"Wait," Jiayang said.

"Wait?" Carlos said. "What the fleek for?"

The bolter fire ceased, replaced by the sound of metal feet slapping the floor surface. The building fell silent. the only sound explosions in the distance.

"Ms. Liu? Are you in there?" a voice said. "Are you alright?"

"I'm fine," Jiayang shouted back.

"Is Michele Carter with you?" the voice asked.

Jiayang locked eyes with Michelle. "Yes, she is."

"You can come out," the voice said. "The area is secure."

"So, this is it," Michelle said.

"You told me to contact him," Jiayang replied.

"What the hell is going on?" Carlos asked.

Michelle stood. "Let's find out."

The three of them walked down the damaged hall, stepping over destroyed bots to the outside. Five UCS transport drones hovered overhead, the ground secured by dozens of UCS agents. A tall man dressed in UCS battle armor approached them, a smile on his brown face. He nodded at Jiayang, then saluted Michelle.

"Captain Lucas Jones," the man said. It's a pleasure to meet you, Ms. Liu. Commander Ghazini sends his regards."

"Thank you, captain," Jiayang said.

The captain approached Michelle.

"It is an honor to meet you, Agent Carter. We thought you were dead. When Ms. Liu informed us you were still alive, it gave us all hope."

Michelle looked dumbfounded. "What?"

"I'll explain on the flight back," Captain Jones said.

The three of them began following the captain when one of the agents placed his hand on Carlos's chest.

"Not you," he said.

"He's with me," Michelle said.

"He's not UCS," the captain said. "This is confidential."

"Carlos goes where I go," Michelle said.

The captain glared at Carlos.

"You heard the agent," Carlos said. "We're a pair."

The captain nodded and the agent relented.

They followed the captain to an awaiting private drone.

"Well, that was exciting," Carlos said.

"We're not in the clear yet," Michelle replied.

"So why are we getting into this drone?" Carlos asked.

"Because it's the only chance you have," Jiayang replied. "If it makes you feel any better, I don't know what's waiting for me at the end of this flight, either."

"We'll know in few hours," Michelle said.

Michelle, Carlos, and Jiayang boarded the drone. The automatic door closed; moments later the drone lifted then streaked into the eastern horizon.

* * *

It had been three years since Michelle wore the UCS uniform. Before, she always felt proud of it, but now the outfit left her unsure. She'd discovered so much since going underground, most of which shook her foundation in the world and destroyed her trust in its institutions. Still, there was a glimmer of hope. She was back at UCS, and no one was trying to kill her. That was a start.

She exited her room on the 17th floor of Newlanta Downtown Regency, striding to the elevator. The door slid open; the lift was full, but the passengers made room. Michelle worked her way to the rear.

An elderly woman looked her up and down then shared a smile with her.

"Thank you for what you do," she said. "The world is safer because of you."

"Thank you," Michelle replied, her chest tightening.

"My great grandparents told me about the Hackers," the old woman said. "They were so brave, like you."

"I wouldn't call myself brave," Michelle replied.

"Of course you wouldn't," the woman said. "Brave people never do."

The lift opened and Michelle quickly exited. Carlos and Jiayang were waiting, Carlos dressed casual yet smart and Jiayang looking as if she'd never missed a beat from corporate leader to luxury prisoner.

"You took your time," Carlos said.

"It was worth it," Jiayang said. "The uniform suits you."

Captain Jones entered the lobby, greeting everyone with a generous smile.

"Good morning," he said. "Are we ready?"

"Can we stop on the way for breakfast?" Carlos asked.

"Of course," the captain replied.

"Then I'm ready!"

They boarded the lift. As promised, the captain requested the lift stop at Mama Lula's for breakfast before they continued to UCS headquarters. Michelle almost wished she hadn't eaten, for her stomach began to churn as she saw the building again. The lift descended to the curbside, and they exited. Captain Jones led them into the building. As they headed to Ghazini's office, the agents shared smiles, salutes, and nods with the trio. Michelle returned the attention despite her nervousness.

"Michelle!"

She turned her head to see Afaafa walking to them, a smile of her face.

"Michelle, it's so good to see you," she said.

She saluted Michelle then gave her a generous hug.

"It's good to see you too, Afaafa," Michelle said. "Sorry about your office."

"No problem," Afaafa replied. "You did what you had to do. Besides, he was the one who broke in."

Carlos stepped to Afaafa, took her hand then kissed it.

"I apologize," he said. "I was just following orders."

Afaafa slowly extracted her hand from Carlos's grip then wiped it on her pants.

"Anyway, I'm glad you're back," Afaafa said to Michelle. "I hope all goes well with Ghazini."

"Thanks," Michelle said. They continued to follow Captain Jones to the elevator.

"Why the fleek did you kiss her hand?" Micelle asked Carlos.

"Because she's fine," he replied. "I thought we had a connection."

"She wiped that connection on her pants," Jiayang said.

"Oh, so now you got jokes?" Carlos replied.

"Not a joke, just an observation." Jiayang looked at Michelle then winked.

They boarded the elevator to the 32nd floor, the suite of Uhuru Ghazini, Head of UCS. The doors opened to a spacious office accented with natural Ficus trees, the walls covered with Neo African paintings and fabrics. Ghazini sat at his mahogany desk playing his holoboard like a concert pianist while his eyes focused on the screen. They had almost reached him before he turned to face them. A smile came to his deep umber fac as he swiped away the keyboard and screen then stood. Ghazini was a head taller than Carlos and half as wide, his UCS uniform fitting his athletic frame snuggly.

"Please, sit," he said as he gestured to the cushioned seats before his desk. "That will be all, captain."

The captain saluted then marched away. Ghazini sat, the smile still on his handsome face.

"It's good to see you again, Jiayang. I thought we'd lost you to the other side."

"You did for a moment," Jiayang replied. "This one talked me into coming back." Jiayang nodded at Michelle.

"I've heard she can be persuasive," Ghazini replied.

"Especially when she has someone hold a bolter to your head," Jiayang said.

"I was just following orders," Carlos said in his defense.

Ghazini turned his attention to Carlos, his smile fading.

"You're a long way from the gutter, aren't you?"

"Hey, that's uncalled for!" Carlos said. "It's because of me Michelle is still alive."

"Is that true?" Ghazini asked Michelle.

"Sort of," she replied.

"If that's the case, I apologize," Ghazini said. "It's because of you that we have a chance to get things back right."

"I don't understand," Michelle said. "I've been running for my life for three fleeking years, and now I'm a hero?"

"You were a hero the day you went rogue," Ghazini said. "You did something the rest of us were either too weak or too afraid to do. You fought back."

Michelle glanced away. "I couldn't let them take my life and my livelihood. That was all I had left. But now I discover everything I was protecting was a scam. How do you explain that?"

"I can't," Ghazini said. "The Hackers decided long ago to compromise. We were left with the aftermath. When the Elites decided to make a move, those who wanted to fight back couldn't. We didn't know who was with them or who wasn't. But the more you resisted, the more they were exposed."

"I could have used some help," Michelle said.

"You received more than you realized," Ghazini replied. "How do you think you survived for three years?"

Michelle shrugged. "I thought I was good."

"You are, but not that good," Ghazini replied.

"So why am I here?" Michelle asked.

Ghazini leaned back into his chair.

"The Vegas operations got us the core of the Elites planning the Takeover," Ghazini said. "But there's a lot more work to do. I'd like your help. I want you to take over our Field Operations Division. You'll oversee finding and apprehending the remaining insurgents."

Michelle's eyes widened. "Are you serious?"

"Deadly serious," Ghazini said.

"Will I have to be in the field?"

"That's your decision,"

"I'll take it."

"Hold up," Carlos said. "You don't know all the details."

"I know enough," Michelle replied. "Besides, you'll be helping me."

"Hey, you're signing up for this, not me."

"I'm hiring you as an independent contractor. You do what you always do. All you have to do is pass anything along that might be useful to me."

Michelle looked to Ghazini for approval, and he nodded.

"That's it?" Carlos asked.

"That's it," Michelle said.

Carlos laughed. "Shit, where do I sign?"

"What about me?" Jiayang asked. "The last time I saw my facility it was being blown to bits."

"I wasn't responsible for that," Ghazini said.

"UCS was," Jiayang replied. "And you run UCS."

"You didn't let me finish," Ghazini said. "The Elites wanted your plant destroyed because they built a more advanced facility to provide them with security and servant A.I. once their takeover was complete. It's in our custody now, and it needs someone to run it."

Jiayang frowned. "I don't work for the government. Not enough money in it."

"It won't be government run," Ghazini said. "It will be run as you see fit. We might require a favor or two from time to time, and of course you'll have to pay proper taxes."

"I was afraid of that," Jiayang said.

"It's your choice," Ghazini said. "You can always start from scratch."

Jiayang extended her hand and Ghazini shook it. She stood.

"I'll be staying in the King on Ponce," she said. "Have the papers sent to my suite."

She looked at Michelle and Carlos.

"It's been a pain," she said. "I hope I never see you two again."

"As long as you behave, you won't," Michelle replied.

Jiayang laughed before leaving the office.

"I guess we should go, too," Michelle said. "You have work to do."

"You do as well," Ghazini replied.

"I have something to do first," Michelle said.

Ghazini nodded. "I understand. We talked to your husband yesterday. He's anxious to see you."

Michelle jumped from her seat and ran to the elevator.

"Hey, wait up!"

Carlos ran after her, catching up just before the elevator doors opened. They both stepped inside.

"Thank you, Carlos," Michelle said.

"Don't mention it," Carlos replied.

Michelle lunged at Carlos, wrapping her arms around him.

"I mean it. Thank you so much."

Carlos hugged her back.

"We're a team," he said.

The elevator doors opened, and they walked fast to the street. Two personals landed at the curbside.

"It's been real," Carlos said.

"It has," Michelle said. "Don't die."

"You, too," Carlos replied.

They climbed into their personals and the doors lowered then shut. The personals rose into traffic, then flew in opposite directions.

About The Author

Milton Davis is an award winning Black Speculative fiction author and owner of MVmedia, LLC, a publishing company specializing in Science Fiction and Fantasy based on African/African Diaspora history, culture, and traditions. Milton is the author of twenty-one novels and short story collections and editor/coeditor of ten anthologies. His short stories have appeared in several anthologies and magazines, most notably Black Panther: Tales of Wakanda, Slay: Stories of the Vampire Noire, Obsidian Literature and Arts in the African Diaspora and Tales from the Magician's Skull. Milton's story 'The Swarm' was nominated for the 2017 British Science Fiction Association Award for Short Fiction and his story, Carnival, was nominated for the 2020 British Science Fiction Association Award for Short Fiction.

Looking for more exciting Cyberfunk action? Look no further than MVmedia!

What is Cyberfunk? It is a vision of the future with an Afrocentric flavor. It is the Singularity without the Eurocentric foundation. It's *Bladerunner* with sunlight, *Neuromancer* with melanin, cybernetics with rhythm.

Nineteen amazing Black Speculative Fiction authors have come together to share their visions on the pages of this book. Prepare to be mesmerized by their stories.

Featuring stories by Eugen Bacon, Zig Zag Clayborne, Gerald L. Coleman, Ashleigh Davenport, Milton J. Davis, Minister Faust, Donovan Hall, John Jennings, Ronald Jones, Nicole Givens Kurtz, Kyoko M, Carole McDonnell, Violette Meier, T.C. Morgan, Balogun Ojetade, Hannibal Tabu, Jarla Tangh, Napoleon Wells, and K. Ceres Wright.

The City anthology is a unique creation. It's a concept anthology, a collection of stories where eighteen different authors share their vision of a single idea. It's Cyberfunk, cyberpunk stories that play with future concepts from an African/African American perspective. Most of all it's engaging, exciting, thought provoking and fun. Like the inhabitants, the City is perceived in various ways by the various writers. Some stories intersect, some diverge, but they all entertain. The result is a journey into a unique world described by unique and engaging voices.